Flight Over the Border

About the author

In this novel of intrigue, the author opens a window on his own experiences. A flying enthusiast himself, he has for the last fifteen years been the West German director of *Christian Mission to the Communist World*, the organisation founded by Pastor Richard Wurmbrand to help Christians who suffer under Communist rule.

Flight over the Border

A Novel

Hans Martin Braun

Dedicated to my children
in the hope that this story will serve as
a stimulus for them to seek the truth.

☆   ☆   ☆

All the characters in this book are fictional
and any resemblance to actual persons is
coincidental. However, the story is
based on historical facts.

Originally published in Germany
under the title Flug über die Grenze

First published in the UK in 1985
by Marshall Morgan & Scott.

British Library Cataloguing in Publication Data

Marc Tasstain was a quiet, reserved sort of person. He spoke only if it was absolutely necessary.

This was exactly the way he reacted on finding out that his older brother Mike had died in a mysterious plane crash. For a long time he went about without saying a word to anyone, waiting till he could investigate the matter further. Marc's brother had never been married, nor had he made many friends. His parents, however, never got over the tragic death. Neither they, nor any other members of the family, knew that Mike Tasstain had been working for the Russian secret service.

Marc himself had had no idea until, after looking through Mike's belongings, he came across something strangely familiar. It was a pair of leather gloves Marc had given to his brother years before as a present. What was so strange was that both thumbs had been cut off. The brothers always used to greet each other by making a fist and pointing their thumbs in the air to show everything was okay. Mike would never have cut off the thumbs if he had not wanted to say something.

Later, when the police tried to play down the cause of the crash, Marc started to suspect that it might have been other than accidental. Since he too was a pilot, he was able to gain access to the records of the official investigation. It was then that he discovered that while the 'official' cause of the crash had been recorded as an engine fault, in reality the Russian secret service had been mixed up in the affair.

'Agent 727 (Tasstain's brother) had been on his way to make contact with the Western secret service.' This Marc was able to learn from an air force pilot friend of his. The mission had been intercepted and Marc's brother disposed of. The sixty-five passengers on board and the three-man crew all lost their lives as the plane, allegedly, exploded.

Marc was positive that his brother had been killed as he tried to flee some act of malice. It was quite beyond him, though, to know why he had fallen prey to the bloodhounds so quickly. And why Mike? There were so many spies working with friend and foe alike who were never removed. So much remained a mystery to him. One thing he did discover, though, was that throughout his life his brother had had one specific goal. Exactly what this was, Marc was not to find out until much later. At the time, however hard he tried, he couldn't find out any more information, and he finally gave up his search for the truth. After all, he reasoned, it was his brother's own fault that it had happened. He should have known what he was getting himself into. Marc was reminded of something his grandfather once said: Whoever runs into the jaw of danger will find himself swallowed up by it.

Still, for a long time he was bothered by the fact that the matter hadn't been cleared up. He and his brother had understood each other especially well, and he was weighed down by his brother's death. Questions about the purpose of life, which had never interested him before, started coming into his head. Often he would sit deep in thought, pondering over the apparent meaninglessness of life. But then duty would call, and he would put away his memories of Mike, and all that they evoked.

☆   ☆   ☆

Marc Tasstain was head of research and development in a factory that made printing machines. In his field, he was respected as a specialist who always excelled. His knack for innovation, his technical skill and ideas for improvements had combined to produce some of the best machines on the market. As a result, he had been invited to join the board of directors. If he wasn't with his engineers, absorbed in some new experiment, he would be working on some technical development or out directing a new installation, or closing a business deal. Wherever the company had an opportunity to open a new contract, he was sure to be there.

It seemed as though he was never idle. The other directors valued his rare talent for being able to master any difficult task. Many departments were always asking him for advice – not only because of his expert knowledge but because of his insight into people and issues. But nobody could call him easy-going. He could be very surly at times, and then his subordinates were only too glad to avoid him.

At that time the company was involved in working out plans for setting up a subsidiary in Russia. Soviet firms had approached management with a suggestion on the manufacture of machine parts for the entire Eastern bloc and Asia. Everything was to be centrally coordinated – planning, construction and execution. Opening up a market in these areas seemed to be a very promising venture, one not to be taken lightly.

It went without saying that the branch office should be constructed according to the most modern standards. Tasstain was put in charge of working out the plans and discussing them with the Soviets, a task which left him with no spare time. His family, of course, suffered the most. Dora Tasstain, a graceful and sensitive woman, tried time and again to get her husband to take it easy.

'Your health can't take the stress and tension for too long, Marc,' she urged him. 'Sit down at least once in a while and spend a bit of time with the children.' She knew that playing with the children brought some measure of calm to his restless soul. When he had the youngest of the four sitting on his knees, he would look at his wife with such a loving expression that she could hardly contain her happiness.

But these times never lasted long. He was always pulled back to his work. He would sometimes stay at the factory all through the night drawing and redrawing plans, energetically exploring the suggestions and possibilities raised by such an important project.

Then the moment came when Tasstain's department was ready to present a complete package of plans, explanations, tenders and analyses. The Soviet delegation could now be invited to visit the factory and discuss the project.

On the afternoon of a somewhat dismal day, Tasstain and his assistant, Dr Ott, stood at the airport awaiting the arrival of their guests from Moscow.

☆　☆　☆

The mission Silvia Schmitz received this time from headquarters was more or less routine, a job that would be over quickly. As she encoded her report on Marc Tasstain, her interest was awakened by the mental image it evoked. There was a note on his friendship with flight pilots and his love of flying. Information on his finances and property was also given. A list of his inventions and patents was included, plus an outline of his career since his military service. He was summed up as having a strong personality, a harmonious family life, and the ability to maintain good business relationships throughout the entire world.

Undoubtedly headquarters would find this information very useful. And she guessed she would probably have a lot more to do on this case. After coding the message Silvia rolled it tightly, opened up a fat ballpoint pen, inserted the paper, and dropped the pen into her handbag.

In many ways she looked like a rather prim school mistress, and she was respected for her straitlaced manner, but this disguised an impish spirit, and she always had a new trick up her sleeve. This was unusual for a member of the secret service but very often came in handy. Her colleagues knew her for her cold-blooded temperament and quick thinking. Outsiders would never have expected such behaviour from this quiet, seemingly timid young lady.

She left her flat on the fourth floor of a high rise block in the centre of the city, and taking an indirect route and a variety of methods of transport, made her way to meet her contact.

At the time scheduled she passed on her report and picked up new instructions. Two pens changed hands without either owner's uttering a sound.

Silvia Schmitz returned home.

☆ ☆ ☆

'That's a really sharp Russian,' Tasstain thought as he shook hands with Mr Orlov and greeted the two newcomers. Orlov, speaking fluent German, introduced his colleague Mr Bugitchkov to Marc. He was a bit smaller than Orlov and somewhat austere. He seemed to be gazing around without interest, but then Marc noticed his eyes. They fixed him with an icy, penetrating stare that made him shudder with horror.

'We have a week for our discussions. I hope that by the end of this time all will be settled,' Orlov said in a friendly but determined tone a few minutes later as they were on their way to their hotel.

'We've taken care of everything here,' Marc

9

answered. 'If you like, we could visit the factory tomorrow and get on with our discussions immediately. We're also expecting a government official who is to take part in the talks right from the beginning. There should be no problem in settling everything within a week.'

He was glad that the Russians themselves had set a limit to the duration of their stay, as the week promised to be very tedious. But it was questionable whether there would be sufficient time to clear up any detailed technical questions.

'We've taken the liberty of preparing a small reception for you tonight in the hotel,' Marc continued. 'You will be able to meet the directors of our factory and those participating in the project. If you have any questions about the project, please feel free to ask them tonight. And we would like you to know that if you need anything at all we are at your disposal the entire time. Dr Ott, my assistant, and I shall be available whenever you need us.'

Orlov thanked the gentlemen for their kindness. His colleague, remote and expressionless, stared coldly as if the matter were totally meaningless to him.

As they pulled up in front of the hotel, Bugitchkov watched the taxi that had been following them drive by and park. Inside was a young lady whose familiar face he was just able to discern. He knew they would soon come in contact with one another.

Deep in thought, Tasstain drove home. He didn't know what to make of the two Russians. It seemed to him that they didn't trust one another at all. Orlov must be the technical expert, whereas Bugitchkov seemed more like a party functionary. Well, he'd find out in due time. Right now it was pointless to worry about it.

Up to now Tasstain hadn't really done much thinking about Eastern countries or their peoples. Their way of life, character, and mode of thought were completely new to him. The Russian visitors had stirred up his curiosity, and he was determined to find out as much as possible from Orlov, who had made the better impression on him. In fact, he promised himself he would get to know this Russian. If he were able to learn more about the nation and its people, he would be able to judge them better and this might help him in his handling of the project.

Back in the office, he passed on his first impressions to his fellow directors and made sure that Dr Ott had taken care of the final preparations in the hotel. Then he went home to get ready for the evening.

✰   ✰   ✰

With its twenty storeys the Continental Hotel stood out proudly among the other buildings in the city. Its illuminated exterior seemed to proclaim the importance of the events inside. Mysteriously a light would blink off and another one on as if to announce the arrival of some important guest.

The visitors from Russia were expected on the fourth floor of the hotel. While Dr Ott was inspecting the rooms for the last time, a knock was heard at the door of room 648. Bugitchkov opened the door. A hotel maid stood facing him. It was Silvia Schmitz. His expression remained unchanged as Silvia asked if there were anything she could do for him. When he asked for cigarettes, she handed him a pack, wished him good evening and disappeared behind the door marked 'Staff only.' Her second mission had been accomplished.

Bugitchkov turned the pack around in his hands a couple of times before taking out a cigarette. Instead of putting it to his lips, he unscrewed the end of the little white tube and extracted a film not much bigger than a credit card. It was impossible to make out its contents with the naked eye. He carefully placed the film between two glass slides and slid it into the back of a camera. By looking through the eyepiece and turning a knob he was able to read the message on the film.

With a satisfied nod of his head, he continued with the remaining tubes, meticulously scrutinising the message on each film he removed. The information on Tasstain was not yet complete but soon would be as they now had the opportunity to take a closer look at his lifestyle. Before leaving for the reception he saw Orlov and passed on the information he had just received.

☆ ☆ ☆

Later in the evening Tasstain and Orlov took their leave of the reception and withdrew to a quiet corner where they were able to enter into deep conversation. They were able to settle a lot of things on this first evening. Many details were discussed and lines of communication were established between specialists in the two companies.

The topic of flying just happened to come up, and Marc, an experienced pilot, discovered in Orlov an interested listener. Stimulated by the Russian's questions, he told of his many flying adventures, of his first flight alone which ended in a crash landing, his exhilarating flight over the Alps, his first night landing, and all his blind flights, many of which took him over vast distances. Orlov's questions went on and on. It seemed he couldn't hear enough of Marc's tales.

'Look,' Marc said, 'how about coming over to the airfield this week with me, and I'll take you up? Then you can see for yourself what it's like.'

Looking off in the distance towards his colleague at the other end of the room, Orlov decided to take Marc up on his offer. They agreed to stick to business the next day and set aside time on the following afternoon to break for a flight.

As they said goodnight, Marc added, 'I'll have you picked up around nine o'clock tomorrow morning for the visit to the factory.'

☆ ☆ ☆

'I've been told to ask you to show the utmost hospitality to our Russian visitors,' Sachs, the government official, explained to the directors for the third time before the Russians arrived. 'It is in our own interest that they receive VIP treatment during their stay. And if there are any difficulties we can help with, you can count on us for any assistance or support. Naturally, we are not so much interested in the business transactions as in our relationship to the Russian nation. We can demonstrate our good will by cooperating in the project. Please keep us informed on everything.'

When the two Russians arrived, they were greeted by the government official and the managing director of the firm. Then they set off to visit the factory.

In the design office, where all the drawings of the planned branch office were hung on a screen, the Russians remained the longest, expressing strong interest in the detailed plans. Tasstain explained all the intricacies at great length.

But no details were given of the machines to be installed. He had been told to be very careful with any information about these machines. He needed no coaching. He had always been discreet about technical data and was especially so now, because he had been working on the design of a new printing machine and had become aware that this machine could revolutionise the printing industry.

He was fully aware of the fact that such a large-scale project as building an entire factory for the Russians could be quite risky. Who would intervene if Soviet officials suddenly took over construction of the factory and said they no longer needed help? And even if the Soviets were forced to rely on the parent company for instructions and advice in the beginning phases, who was to stop them from taking over after a period of time? Even government officials would be useless then!

Tasstain tore himself away from such thoughts. Nothing would be accomplished that way. He decided to reveal only what was necessary, but at the same time to behave as though the Russians were loyal business partners who would abide by their contracts. Orlov, in any case, had made a good impression on him. Surely he would be able to talk over his concern with him before the final contract was signed.

☆　☆　☆

In addition to Tasstain, only Dr Ott, Tasstain's technical assistant, and the mechanic Wilhelm Range, had any knowledge of the new design. Tasstain knew Range from his military service days in the air force and had asked the loyal flight mechanic to work with him in the factory. All three in this team had become good friends, Tasstain being the brilliant designer, Dr Ott the cool calculator, and Wilhelm Range the constructor who – on occasion at least – brought to reality some incredible new design.

Range, who was in charge of the factory's work-shops, was known for his sensible matter-of-factness. A loner, he often appeared strange to others. Tasstain once observed him kneeling in front of his work bench. He quickly left without Range's noticing him, and never mentioned a word to anyone about what he had seen. But he assumed that Range's behaviour had some reason behind it and wondered what it might be.

But any task Range tackled was carried out with utmost care. The construction of the new machine was obviously in the best hands.

Every night, after the regular crew had left the premises, Range continued working on the machine, which stood half-finished in a well-locked room in the cellar underneath the workshops. Any special parts he was unable to manufacture he ordered with precise specifications from the manufacturing plant of the firm. Once they arrived, he took care to install them himself. Frequently, when time allowed, Tasstain came into the cellar to supervise the construction and whenever necessary lent a helping hand.

Today, Range had decided to go home earlier than usual. By five in the afternoon he was already sitting in the canteen. Since he lived alone, he had made the factory his home. He knew every inch, every machine, and almost every face. The new waitress who brought him his food thus automatically caught his eye. She had the features of a governess and a couple of mischievous dimples at the corners of her mouth.

☆ ☆ ☆

When Tasstain arrived at the airfield with Dr Ott and the two Russians, his machine had already been tanked up and rolled out of the hangar on to the taxi strip. The olive-green Cessna 210, a six-seater with a single engine, glowed in the midday sun. The compact little high-wing monoplane was quite deceptive. What it lacked in streamlining it made up for in power. The plane possessed an extraordinary climbing capacity and was very comfortable to fly.

Tasstain, busy checking under the hood of the engine, turned to his flight companions. 'If it's all right with you, we'll first of all make a five-minute test flight close to the landing field. That way you'll be able to tell if you feel okay or not and can then decide if you'd like to continue or return to the hangar.'

The Russians never allowed each other out of their sight and this was beginning to get on Marc's nerves. So he was scheming to get Orlov to himself by the simple strategy of making Bugitchkov want to cut short his ride. He had thought out an appropriate flight routine. Wind conditions were ideal for what he had in mind. At twenty-five to thirty knots a gusty wind swept the runway from the side, not ideal when taking up passengers for the first time.

Dr Ott, who sensed what Tasstain's intentions were, kept discreetly still and stayed by the hangar ready to receive the hapless victim. While Bugitchkov looked grave and somewhat dyspeptic, Orlov had a difficult time concealing his excitement.

With a low purring of its engine the machine rolled on to the runway. After Tasstain had made sure his passengers had fastened their straps, he went through his checklist of all the instruments and controls, brought the machine to a halt, and waited to receive the all-clear-for-take-off signal.

'Delta Echo November Mike India,' barked ground control over the radio, 'runway 24 ready to go. Take off as you please. Bear to the right after takeoff. Nice flight, Marc!'

'Thanks, Tom.' Marc moved the throttle into start position. With a loud whine the high-wing plane gathered speed along the bumpy runway, lifted off the ground after about eighty yards, and quickly gained altitude.

Pulling in the landing gear, Marc noticed how strong the winds were gusting from his left. With a slight grin he steered into the next gust with more force than was absolutely necessary. The plane leaned with a sudden jerk towards the left wing as if bowing to the control tower, then was set aright again as another gust whipped across the frail craft, causing it to shake as if it, too, were enjoying the fun. Bugitchkov, growing paler by the minute, was thrown back and forth in his seat. He looked down apprehensively and seemed to be considering a return to terra firma.

Meanwhile, Tasstain was careful to explain everything he was doing during the ascent. 'Landing gear pulled in engine rpms throttled by 200, boost pressure of the propeller set. As soon as we have climbed to 3,000 feet we'll maintain that altitude. Then it ought to be calmer,' he said, looking back over his shoulder at his passengers. With the help of the vertical rudder, he allowed the plane to be jerked again, causing Bugitchkov to inhale sharply and roll his eyes nervously.

Within minutes they had reached 3,000 feet. Banking to the left and raising the nose to what seemed an almost vertical position, Marc circled the airfield, giving his distinguished passengers a clear view of the runway and control tower, which resembled mere toys on a carpet of green. Bugitchkov, certain by now that they were going to tip over, was quite obviously not enjoying the scenery.

When the next gust of wind forcefully lifted the plane skyward, his will surrendered. By now he was ashen. When Tasstain, suddenly taking note of his discomfiture, asked if he wanted to continue the flight, he shook his head decidedly. '*Nyet.*'

17

Even Orlov could not restrain a grin as he watched Tasstain maintain his composure as he prepared to land. Again he described every step.

'Propeller set for descent, at 130-mile velocity, wing flaps at ten degrees, trim the engine.' Now the plane was in an angle of descent, lined up directly for the runway. The strong gusts continued and counter manoeuvres were still necessary. Tasstain positioned the nose of the plane into the wind and cut the power as they landed somewhat unsteadily on the runway.

For Bugitchkov it was not a minute too soon. Thoroughly queasy, he almost fell on the ground in his haste to disembark and barely maintained his self-control as he made for the airport building and lurched inside. Dr Ott's offer of a short drink on the terrace went unheeded.

Again Tasstain could scarcely repress a grin as he taxied to the runway for the second ascent. They quickly reached 3,000 feet, then continued their flight just beneath the clouds. Wisps of cloud brushed swiftly across their path, appearing and disappearing like wraiths into the greyness above.

The landscape below looked like a giant jigsaw. Winding rivers were ribbons of silver lace scattered over the green countryside, and the red roofs of villages were tiny handfuls of red gravel.

'It's a new experience for me,' Orlov admitted, 'and I'm very grateful to you for giving me such an opportunity.'

'Oh, it's a real pleasure for me to have aroused someone's interest in flying,' Tasstain rejoined with enthusiasm. He switched on the automatic pilot to a radio beacon fifty miles away, turned the time dial of his clock to the planned flight time, and prepared to give his full attention to Orlov.

'As a businessman I've always found that the best

results are achieved by being as frank as possible,' Marc declared, opening up the conversation. 'Maybe in your country it isn't possible to deal in such a manner, but I wanted to make it clear to you that you can put your complete trust in me in that respect.'

Orlov hesitated, then looked Tasstain straight in the eye and said, 'If I were you I'd do exactly the same. But business objectives in my country are not the same as in yours. So your rules do not apply to us.'

As if he had already said too much, he suddenly went silent. He wondered whether he should have said more about the future victory of the proletariat, the world revolution, or the successful communist economy. In his work, only pioneer tasks like this one, the construction of a new factory unlike any known before to his country, had engaged his interest. Every time he started working on a new plant, it was an exciting adventure for him. From the first use of the caterpillar tractor to the operation of machinery in production, he was continuously on the spot to witness every stage of planning. It gave him great satisfaction to have a say in how and when a new factory was to be built.

And the ends justified the means; he would use everything within the scope of his power. He never made it a point to ask where blueprints, drawings or patents came from. He was smart enough to hide his lack of interest in political issues, and even had a certain way with party functionaries and exerted a lot of influence in the Ministry of Economy in his country.

When it came to Tasstain, however, it was not easy for Orlov to maintain his normal stance. He had ascertained that he was not simply dealing with another opportunist or capitalist who was merely after money. There seemed to be something of greater value to the man. Perhaps he, too, had pioneer

19

instincts and loved making new discoveries for his country. This helped bring the two closer together in spirit.

'I hope, in any case, that fruitful cooperation will arise out of this project and as far as possible I will return your gesture of frankness,' Orlov said, trying to keep their talk brief.

For the moment Tasstain was content. More words would not have carried any more conviction. And he had traced a certain sincerity in Orlov's responses. He was sure that other opportunities would arise when he would be able to find out the true intentions of the Soviets. Then, too, there was still a lot of time before contracts were due to be signed.

Just then they flew over the set radio beacon. Tasstain banked the plane in a swinging loop on to a return course and brought the craft down to an altitude of fifty feet. As they flew close to the ground, Orlov was able to see the hilly landscape roll by as if on an assembly line. With the setting sun behind them, they watched their shadow guide their path ahead, gliding swiftly over woods, villages, and hills. Could it be a symbol of their future cooperation, of the ease with which they would sweep over all obstacles in their path?

☆　☆　☆

The instructions Silvia Schmitz received from Bugitchkov a day before the Russians' departure were perfectly clear. In the usual manner she was to gather information on major processes in the factory, technical details on the machines to be employed and on the talks held by the executives concerning the machines and financial matters.

As waitress in the canteen of the factory, she had

been busy setting up her work field and had already made friendly contacts with many employees and workers. She had also found out where the waste-paper baskets of the directors were emptied and from discarded memos she had already been able to piece together some interesting information. As a result, Silvia was optimistic and had promised to furnish further data very soon.

Headquarters in Moscow had notified her that she would be on the case for a longer period of time and should take the utmost care. The Soviet Ministry of Economy wanted to be kept up to date, but not at the risk of jeopardising this important project.

Silvia Schmitz knew her job well. She was an expert in industrial espionage, and had the back-up of the latest electronic espionage equipment. She found it unfortunate that she had to meddle in the private affairs of Marc Tasstain, but told herself that it was all part of her job. Not a single soul had any idea of the secrets this wolf was hiding under her meek sheep's clothing.

☆   ☆   ☆

'Well, they're on their way back to Moscow,' Marc commented, heaving a sigh of relief as he returned home after taking the Russians to the airport. The evening before, Bugitchkov and Orlov had presented their gifts and given their assurance that soon a message would be arriving from Moscow. Then most certainly exchange visits would be arranged leading up to the signing of the contracts.

·   The handshake between Orlov and Tasstain was more than cordial, and the best wishes they both sent each other as they went their separate ways were more than simple courtesy.

'I'm looking forward to your visit in the Soviet Union,' Orlov shouted before disappearing into the area marked 'Passengers only'.

Tired but content, Marc kissed his wife and said, 'Now you're all going to see a lot more of me. If your mother can look after the children for a couple of days, we can take a drive into the mountains and get a bit of rest.' She hugged her husband in delight. She knew that after a long period of absence he always made it up to her by thinking up something special, and she cherished him all the more for that.

She looked at his tired face and sagging shoulders. For months she had been observing the increasing effects of job pressures and worries. The constant responsibility for the project with Russia, along with his duties in the factory, and finally the strenuous meetings of the past week had exhausted him. He had earned his rest.

☆　☆　☆

The cellar of a Moscow suburban house was gradually filling up with people. At short intervals people scurried through the door, took their seats on the benches that had been placed in the room, and waited in silence. It was quite some time before all the seats were occupied. Eventually the aisles filled up and the room was packed with about a hundred people. The air became heavy and oppressive, yet nobody spoke. The atmosphere was clandestine, expectant.

All of a sudden a music filled the silence. The cellar arches seemed hardly able to contain the singing of a many-voiced choir. Among the light sopranos were rich bass voices suggestive of the vast steppes of Mother Russia. The room resounded with devotion to God.

It was a meeting of Russian underground Christians, who had come from many different parts of the city. They had all joined this illegal congregation because either their church had been destroyed or they were not allowed to follow their Christian faith publicly.

On this occasion a rather unusual circumstance had brought the congregation together. Anatoli Kovlenko, one of the elders, had just been released from prison. Four times he had been arrested and sent either to a work camp or into prison. Altogether he had spent seventeen years behind bars and barbed wire. Never in all those years had the name of one single member of the congregation slipped past his lips, and never had he lost faith in his religion or his God.

During his last sentence he was made to pay dearly for his perseverance; he had been tortured with sound waves until his hearing was almost gone. Only when someone shouted in his ear was he able to understand.

Kovlenko sat erect among the congregation. The fifty-year-old had snow-white hair and sunken eyes. Yet from his face emanated a certain strength. Whoever saw him knew that Kovlenko was a determined man who believed in the cause.

As soon as the psalms had ended, the released prisoner took his Bible, stood up and started reading aloud: 'Praise the Lord, O my soul, and forget not all his benefits...' Those were the words he had chosen for his sermon. He spoke of the good, although he himself had experienced only the bad. Kovlenko beseeched the listeners to hold on to their faith in God and not to allow themselves to be swayed by atheistic propaganda. He warned them all to beware of any indiscreet remarks concerning their clandestine meetings. He then bade farewell to his fellow-believers, shaking the hand of each member of the congregation. Many of those present were crying and embraced the older man with love and admiration, fully aware that he had suffered for them too.

These meetings of the underground church were fraught with danger, especially for the leaders. There was the constant risk that the secret police would show up, and hearings and arrests were common. For this reason all the meetings were convened under some pretext or other, which could be stated in case of emergency.

Things did not always work out as planned. In Kovlenko's case, for instance, the KGB had prepared so much information against him that they automatically had some grounds for taking him into custody. Every package or postcard he received from some relative abroad could be twisted to connect him to the foreign foe. Any number of suspicious contacts from his military service, as well as confessions made by friends and acquaintances, could also be used against him. Since Kovlenko and his comrades in the congregation were not people who would deliberately disobey official authorities, except when forced to do so in order to continue their illegal Christian worship, their situation was tragic.

Twelve men had remained behind in the cellar. They sat around a large table in the corner of the room. This time their talk was about a daring yet dangerous undertaking. One of them was to leave the country as quickly as possible to call the attention of the West to the dire situation they and other congregations were in. For they were sure that there were church-related and humanitarian institutions that would side with their case and help to lessen their suffering, even if they were unable to do away with Russia's religious intolerance. If only they could win the support of others they would surely be able to gain more religious freedom.

Many acts of repression, many arrests, hearings, and other penalties had had to be endured before the members of the congregation were willing to build up this resistance force. The turning point had come when they were forbidden to raise their children in the Christian religion. Unwilling to comply, they had started to give secret religious instruction. But in the state schools, this covert parental teaching was easily detected as the children were confronted with insidious questions. And so those children who had received a Christian upbringing were quickly singled out and their parents threatened. They were told that their children would be placed in reform schools if they refused to abandon this instruction. After many families had been hurt and torn apart, they decided their only way out was to plead with the free Christian world for help. They could not ignore or forsake their Christian belief and education; experience had taught them that this led only to a false peace, and a bad conscience.

'Someone has to break out of this prison!' One of the participants was no longer able to hold back his feelings. The huge fist of the black-bearded, hot-headed Sorvas hammered upon the table, so that the entire group jumped. 'And Kovlenko is the only person suitable for the task,' he growled. 'Do you want to wait until they send us all to the Gulag and stand by idly watching as they take your children away from you and corrupt them with their plans for a Communist revolution? It's a crying shame that we can come to no decision. It's high time someone went and revealed this scandalous, inhuman treatment to the rest of mankind.'

Sorvas wanted to serve God. He longed to pick up a sword and fight for the cause, as Peter had done in the Garden of Gethsemane when his Lord Jesus had been bound and led away. One glance from Kovlenko made him go silent.

'Well,' came the rejoinder, 'I've been able to understand this much, that you want to send a worn-out decrepit man to carry out the task of a young man. What's more, all the authorities will recognise me. That would endanger the mission right from the start.' For Kovlenko, leaving the congregation meant treason. He would rather have been put behind bars than run away.

'Of course, it's only possible with false documents,' another participant added. 'The 'Stranger' wants to have time to plan everything carefully as soon as we make the decision.' Who this Stranger was he failed to mention. But everyone seemed to know and refrained from posing any further questions.

That they intended to attempt an escape out of the tightly sealed country was a sign of strong faith. The leaders of the congregation called it faith in God. No one had ever heard of such an escape coming off. The elders all agreed that Kovlenko was the only one who could be considered for the mission. Besides his mother tongue, Russian, he also spoke fluent German and had distinguished himself as a convincing speaker. Beyond that, as a result of his long years in prison and in the Gulag, he would be a living example of the injustice that was allowed to take place every day in their country.

The elders also knew that Kovlenko would not agree to their plan. And so they had decided to impart their decision as an irrevocable command. That would be the only way he would agree to go.

Now all the others seemed to come alive and tried to persuade Kovlenko with urgent tones and gestures. He would not be leaving any family behind, and precisely because he was older and more experienced, as well as articulate, he would be able to carry out the mission better than any of the others.

Kovlenko was to take a large number of documents with him to the West. These concerned the arrests of the past months, the inhuman treatment in the camps, and a list of people who had been forcibly put into insane asylums. The passport numbers of those concerned, their names and other important information had already been collected, as well as the names of the hearing officers and judges. This had all been photographed on microfilm and, as soon as the journey was arranged, was to be sewn into pieces of clothing. With this information it should then be easy to open up the eyes of the world.

Kovlenko did all he could to oppose the project. During his period of detention he had often contemplated the idea of living in a free country. Fellow prisoners had vividly described to one another what freedom in other parts of the world must be like. But his primary goal was to care for the spiritual needs of the congregation.

Observing how serious the elders were about their demands, he decided to give the matter further thought and prayer. Somehow he had to come to peace with himself. The opinions of those who worried about him and of the congregation were not to be tossed aside lightly.

☆   ☆   ☆

Bugitchkov's department usually dealt only with reconnaissance work at the higher levels. Most of his officials were inside the state factories with instructions to spy on the directors and heads of departments, play them off against one another, dig up subversive ideas, or uncover conspiracies. If no such evidences could be found, they were simply invented. Bugitchkov was a master at his profession.

A short time before, his crew had run across an apparently ordinary theft that did not quite fit into their scheme of things.

On the outskirts of the city a large quantity of cut

sheets of paper had been found in a garage. The consignment was not contained in any of the lists of paper delivered by the nearby paper factory.

Since Bugitchkov at first had no real interest in questioning everyone around the factory, he gave orders for the garage to be put under constant surveillance. Any person who entered the garage and went near it was to be recorded.

There was someone who knew all about the paper – Sorvas, the blackbeard. He worked as a truck driver for the factory and had laid the paper aside. It was to be used for printing Bibles and Psalm books, the possession of which – to say nothing of their manufacture – was strictly forbidden. But as the underground Christians could not do without them, they had set up their own printing press, which, however primitive, still covered their most urgent need for books. In addition, they were printing monthly magazines which were circulated in tens of thousands, under the greatest of risks, to other congregations.

Sorvas was in charge of supplying the necessary paper. Up to now his undertakings had always gone well, but he knew that any small error could make the whole project blow up in his face. Privately he had always expected to be found out and attributed the success to good fortune – or, as he explained to the elders, to the will of God. Since they were God's Bibles being printed for his church, shouldn't God be interested in securing the paper? There was no other possibility of finding paper. The authorities saw reactionary intentions behind any unexplained orders and anyway, the underground congregation had no legal right to procure paper since it was not registered.

Sorvas was also the connecting link with other congregations. With his ingenuity and his company truck, which he drove during the daytime through the countryside, he was able to go about unnoticed, and make important contacts with other congregations, supplying them, too, with what they needed. After a while such a good communication system had been set up between the congregations that some inter-regional contact between churches was able to develop.

Sorvas was able to grasp a situation at a glance and could smell the smoke of a threatening fire. This was now the case. He had the feeling that something was wrong with this shipment of paper that had been put aside and for that reason left it where it was. Although the paper could have been put to good use, the black-bearded man did not rush matters. He could act as fast as lightning if need be, but he also possessed the patience of Job.

☆　☆　☆

When Orlov received approval for the entry of a single-engine sports plane into the USSR, together with the official order to invite a delegation from the German machine factory to come for further talks, he was overjoyed. This project must be of special importance to the Ministry, or his request about the plane, which must have seemed quite strange to them, would surely not have been granted. Now he would be able to prepare a surprise for Tasstain, who would probably not expect such an honour.

Orlov felt closer to that man than he really wanted to admit. Personal feelings had always been taboo with him, and the reserved manner he had taken on in his years of work never permitted him to enter into personal relationships, even if they were purely social or intellectual.

But he felt the need to do something special. He

could not help smiling as he imagined the reserved Tasstain unexpectedly receiving permission to make such an unusual flight.

After signing the invitation, he added a few personal words for Tasstain and put it in the envelope, together with the flight permit.

The visit of the delegation was to take place in the near future. First of all, a thorough discussion of the contents of the contract was on the agenda, and then, if both parties could not come to an agreement on the essentials, they were to visit the construction site near Moscow where the factory was to be built. Following that, Orlov planned further talks with Russian specialists, who were to take over the executive functions in the factory at a later time. A visit to a similar production site was also part of the visitors' programme, as well as participation in cultural events. As usual, every tiny detail, up to the last taxi ride, had been meticulously worked out.

As in the case of all economic enterprises of this kind, the secret service was involved in the preparations for the visit. Bugitchkov's department was working overtime. All those who might come in contact with the visitors were being screened and secretly observed – not a small task. At Orlov's suggestion, the paper factory was to be visted, which meant that virtually the entire staff had to be put under surveillance. And since the case of the unexplained storage of paper had not yet been cleared up, the network of observers was even more complex.

☆   ☆   ☆

Sorvas had long ago noticed that something was brewing in the factory. Many of his colleagues had been called in on various pretences for questioning by management. And the matter of the paper started to gnaw at him, to the point where he decided to ask the Stranger for assistance.

This was complicated, because the Stranger was not the easiest of people to get hold of. In fact, he was very secretive. The only thing anyone knew about him was that he was willing to help dissidents whenever possible. He had been nicknamed 'Stranger' because he practically never showed up himself but passed on his instructions secretly. No one knew his real name. He was truly a stranger to all, including those who might have seen him somewhere. Even Sorvas, who was quick to make friends, was not allowed to grow close to him.

Once, on meeting the Stranger, he had been impressed that behind the expressionless eyes there lay a willingness to help, almost a tenderness, but still he felt uncomfortable in the man's presence. However, since the reclusive man had helped him many times to get out of difficult spots, his shyness had turned into respectful gratitude.

In order to make contact with the Stranger, he first had to get in touch with his wife, a task that necessitated his finding the priest Alexander, who was the key figure in the underground church movement in Moscow. Alexander headed a half-broken-down Orthodox church and its congregation in the northern part of the city; it reminded Sorvas of his own suffering church.

No one would have guessed what sort of function this priest was fulfilling. He looked like a superannuated saint. In his wrinkled face only the eyes seemed to be alive. Like needles they pierced the countenance of the black-bearded man for an instant, then with a certain indifference looked straight ahead again.

'Tell me, when is your next mass to take place?' Sorvas asked. 'The evening mass,' he added, sensing the priest's reluctance to ` reply. That was the password.

'Tomorrow evening,' the priest answered silently, mouthing the words with his lips. Then he shuffled back inside the old church.

Sorvas had learned enough. The next night he would seek out the Stranger's wife among the congregation. No doubt the priest would be able to notify her before then.

Crouching low to gain entry into the tiny room behind the church, he was hardly able to make out the congregation in the dim light. Above the makeshift altar hung a lamp which gave off a feeble yellow glow. Adjusting to the light he saw a face turn toward him in the last row and recognised Natasha. Two clear eyes, in which goodness and beauty vied for expression, met his gaze for an instant, before looking back at the altar.

Sorvas sat down next to Natasha and remained silent for a while. She was a most important person in her own right, but not conspicuously so. He sensed, quite simply, that she could master any situation and make the best out of what was all too often the worst. To him, with his practised constraint, she seemed sometimes unbelievably open. This apparent naiveté, which could easily have landed her in trouble, had constantly led to unexpected and positive results. It was strange, the influence she could have over someone, for she frequently seemed clumsy and even a little scared, and was generally patronisingly dismissed as 'a devout soul'. For this reason no one bothered to put any burdens on her or make undue demands – though from time to time she surprised everyone with some unexpected achievement.

'I have to speak to the "Stranger" as soon as possible,' Sorvas said abruptly. He made it a habit not to ask personal questions, especially about her husband, in case they were overheard.

She nodded her head, ever so slightly. 'I'll ask him.' Then, with concern, 'Is Kovlenko back?'

'He arrived last Sunday,' Sorvas whispered, 'and we want him to leave the country as soon as possible. But there is something in the paper factory I want the Stranger to help me with. Please tell him that it's urgent. They're planning something that I have a strange feeling about.'

'He'll call you. Give my best wishes to Kovlenko.' Natasha stood up and, with head bowed, proceeded toward the front where she lit a candle. Sorvas got up and quietly left.

Two days later he was standing face to face with the Stranger. He explained his apprehension about the paper and outlined the plans of his congregation.

'Don't worry about the paper. I'll take care of that. Just wait until I tell you it's safe to transport it. As for Kovlenko, I'm not quite sure yet if I can help you to get him out of the country. If such a plan is to be successful it has to be thought out very carefully. Speak to no one about it. I'll see what can be done.' A quick handshake, and Sorvas was dismissed.

He was certain the matter was now in good hands. Above all, something had to be done about the paper. In the factory, the controls and investigations had been increased noticeably, and strange faces appeared everywhere. All the problems and wrinkles that had existed for years were now being ironed out.

The feelings of the workers fluctuated between fear and suspense.

☆   ☆   ☆

Already a little late for the directors' meeting, Tasstain rushed down the wide corridor to the conference room and nearly ran into a waitress, who was just coming out of the lift with a tray full of coffee cups. With a mischievous grin, she watched as he narrowly avoided a collision and stumbled to regain his balance.

In his astonishment, Tasstain quickly inspected this slim girl. 'You seem to be new here,' he said, a bit perturbed. 'Where are you heading with all those cups?'

'To the conference room,' she replied, making a polite curtsy. Tasstain pointed her in the right direction, then hastily made his way around the next corner to his destination, where Dr Ott was waiting for him.

'They're all present and waiting for you,' he said, hurrying Tasstain through the open door. Then he signalled to the waitress, who was just coming down the hall. 'This way, please. The men are expecting their coffee.' While she was still serving them, the directors started discussing the forthcoming visit to the Soviet Union.

It was decided to send a delegation of five. Since the major issues would involve the financial aspects of the project, and since the government was to sponsor the entire transaction, the commercial manager of the factory and Sachs the government official, were put in charge of the delegation. For any matters concerning the construction, an architect working closely with the factory was chosen to go along. Tasstain was to take care of all the technical matters. The delegation was rounded out with an interpreter, who had also been provided by the government.

The financing of the project was to consist partly of a government loan, partly capital finance from the factory itself, and partly underwriting by the Soviet government, all of which made the matter quite complicated. Little wonder, then, that Tasstain, who had no interest whatsoever in financial matters, found it difficult to concentrate. In his thoughts he was already in Russia, carrying out the first steps necessary for construction at the new site. He found himself imagining the people he would be working with and picturing the problems he might come across. Then his thoughts wandered to the great Russian steppes, a landscape he was longing to know for himself. Of course, what delighted him most was the thought of flying over this intriguing foreign land. This would certainly provide his restless mind with new adventures and excitement.

'Mr Tasstain, I believe we are still missing the documents on the machines to be installed.' The voice of the sales director shook him out of his reverie. As a matter of fact, he had left them in his office.

'Dr Ott, would you mind getting them for me?' He turned to his assistant, who apparently had been waiting for just that instruction. He promptly got up and left the room. In the meantime, Tasstain explained that it had been estimated that at least two million pounds would be needed to equip the new factory with machinery – probably more. 'We shouldn't be penny-pinching about a factory which is to be fully automated.'

When Dr Ott returned, Tasstain noticed that something was wrong, but he went on speaking as he accepted the file. Meanwhile, Ott sat down and scratched something on a piece of paper, which he then handed to Tasstain: 'Range has something important to tell you. He's waiting in my office.'

Tasstain excused himself for a moment and followed Dr Ott into his office near the conference room. Range stood at the window holding a small object in his hand.

'I found this in our basement,' he said, holding out a tiny aluminium capsule. 'I saw one of these things once before when we had visitors from Japan and the gentlemen took pictures with their minicameras. The film for such a camera comes in a little aluminium capsule like this. I remember how these things were found all over the premises at that time.'

Tasstain turned the tiny object between his two fingers. 'And you mean this could be something important?'

'How else can I explain how this thing got into the basement?' He had always kept the room especially clean, primarily because he often had to work with the tiniest of parts, which got lost very easily. 'Someone must have got into the basement, that's clear enough. And incredible though it may be, they also took photographs.'

Neither of the men wanted to contradict Range, and it was difficult to believe that he could be telling anything but the truth. It was unlikely that he would have jumped to such a critical conclusion without good reason. 'I've not yet made a thorough search because I wanted to tell you as quickly as possible. I did take a closer look at the doors leading to the basement but could find no sign of a break-in. Nothing.'

Tasstain thought for a moment. 'Have you got someone we could trust to put a guard there?'

'I intend to set up my own bed there. Maybe I'll be able to find out something that way. There is someone who could relieve me.'

'For the moment, that is the best we can do,' Dr Ott commented. 'Fortunately no plans were left downstairs. If there really was someone interested in the machine, then they were only able to photograph one that was half-finished.'

'What do you mean, "If there really was someone interested"?' Range was slightly irritated. 'Don't you believe me when I say that someone *was* down there?'

Tasstain intervened, promising Range that he would come down directly after the meeting to take care of everything. Then he hurried back with Dr Ott to the conference room.

☆   ☆   ☆

The incident caused Tasstain quite a few headaches. While he was preparing for the forthcoming visit to the Soviet Union, questions continued to plague him. Who would be interested in this new development? And above all, how had this strictly confidential information leaked out? He scarcely dared think of espionage. Was there perhaps some other good reason for interest in this new discovery? Meanwhile, he had secretly arranged to have the building containing the critical room placed under surveillance. For the period of his absence at least, everything would be taken care of.

Previously he had asked Range to accompany him on his trip to the Soviet Union. Despite the incident, he held to his decision, since he thought the flight mechanic might be of some help during the trip. Beyond that, he thought it might be well for Range to take a look at the proposed site for the machinery. He would then be much better able to supervise its assembly in the factory.

The other members of the team refused to take up Tasstain's offer to fly with him. But he was glad about their decision, as he would then have more time to enjoy the flight and the scenery below. He bent over the flight chart and with his finger traced out the route he would have to take. It led him over Sweden, southern Finland, and over Leningrad to Moscow. As soon as he had measured the distance between any two points, he recorded them on the proper form. Then he recorded the radio beacons he would follow, the course itself, and the flight time necessary for each leg of the journey. With this data he had a good idea of the entire flight and would be able to make the necessary preparations much more quickly and easily.

Particularly important for international air traffic were the estimated flight and arrival times. He assumed that the Russian authorities would want exact specifications. And his planning must not leave any questions unanswered. Altogether the flight was to take six hours, in two three-hour legs. In view of this, it was important to make exact preparations regarding maintenance and refuelling.

On the eve of his departure, Tasstain sat at home sorting out the papers he would need for the talks in Moscow. Then he decided to organise all his maps and charts. As he tried to take his chart case out of the telephone table, something got in the way. Annoyed, he pressed down on the case and carefully slipped it out of the cabinet. Then he reached in and feeling around with his fingers discovered an object no bigger than a matchbox, which had been fastened underneath the top shelf of the cabinet.

His curiosity now thoroughly aroused, he got a knife and with a little effort prised the strange object loose. It lay heavy in his hand, and as he examined it he noticed that it had tiny pin-prick holes on one side. With a screwdriver he loosened the only visible screw and was then able to remove a little metal plate. Awe-struck, he stared down at the contents of the little tin box: it was a tiny microphone. He thought of the devices, similar but somewhat larger, that he was using in his new printing machine.

Only gradually did he become aware of the meaning of this discovery. A microphone inside his private study! How could such a thing happen?

'Dora!' he shouted urgently.

'For heaven's sake, be quiet! The children are

asleep.' His wife was already running down the stairs. 'If you still want to go out tonight, you'll have to be a bit quieter.'

Just as he was about to ask who had been in his study, he came back to his senses. His wife was always a bit fearful when he was away and it would be better if she were not alarmed about what he had discovered. He suppressed his excitement and casually asked, 'Has anyone been around in the past few days – I mean from the company – to give me anything?'

'From the company? No, I'm pretty sure no one has stopped by.'

'Hmm.' He looked down in front of him, momentarily absorbed in his own thoughts. 'Well, I'll just give Dr Ott a brief call. In the meantime you get ready so we can go out for a bite to eat.' After she left, he phoned his assistant, informed him that he had something important to discuss with him before he left on his flight, and asked him to come to the airfield the next morning.

It was with mixed feelings that Marc took his wife out to dinner. He had always made it a habit to do something special for her before going off on a business trip, and he really wanted to savour these farewell moments. But it was difficult for him to enjoy himself on this occasion. His wife found it hard to capture his attention. She talked about the children, told of the mischief the youngest had recently got into, chatted about her shopping and the neighbours and the future dinner invitations. But he scarcely noticed her bubbling cheerfulness, which he usually cherished so much in her.

The thought of the microphone weighed heavily on his mind. Could it somehow tie in with the discovery in the factory? He had a gut feeling that it had something to do with the project. And of course any connection with the transaction with the Soviet

Union could not be excluded. The whole matter became increasingly mysterious, almost uncanny. He frowned slightly.

'You're not really listening to anything I've been saying,' Dora chided. Half worried, half offended, she laid her hand on Marc's arm. 'These are the last hours we'll be spending together for weeks. You really should try to shut out all those thoughts of business.' She brightened, acting the part of the caring wife. 'We don't want to stay up too late before your strenuous flight tomorrow. I know it'll be extremely trying for you this time. Let's go home and get some rest. Actually, I'm pretty tired myself.'

The suggestion came as a relief, and Marc was grateful for her consideration. No one, he thought, has Dora's intuitive ability to know exactly what a person needs at a given moment.

But this time Dora's cheerfulness was only a thin veneer. She had noticed that something was wrong – in fact she had never seen Marc so upset. The prospect of the trip to Russia made her ill at ease. She decided to speak to Dr Ott about it within the next couple of days.

☆　☆　☆

The following morning, as Tasstain climbed into the cockpit, he realised that he was in no condition for the flight. All night long he had tossed and turned, going over and over in his mind the meaning of the two discoveries and trying to decide what course of action to follow. Everything had happened so suddenly, and time was definitely not on his side. The best he could do was explain the circumstances to Dr Ott and instruct him to get in touch with one of his friends in the Ministry of Defence for advice. Beyond that, he made him promise to post an inconspicuous watchman in front of the house during his absence. He shuddered to think what might happen while he was away. Everything seemed to be aimed at him personally, or at least at his discovery. At any rate, it eased his mind to know that his family was being looked after.

Range was busy stowing away the luggage while Marc went through the final checks. He had submitted his flight plan, and in twenty-five minutes they would take off.

As the Cessna rolled to its starting position, Marc raised his hand to wave goodbye to Dora and Dr Ott, who were standing at the edge of the field. Applying full throttle, he guided the plane down the runway, then lifted off imperceptibly into a gentle breeze, mindful that he was carrying less than a third of his permitted weight. He ascended easily to three thousand feet, then called the control tower. After about three minutes an answer finally came and he was able to transmit his first radio message: 'Delta Echo November Mike India started at 0840 hours, altitude 3,000 feet, position five miles south of Charly. Request clearance for instrument flying to Stockholm. Over.'

Planes arriving from smaller airports were a rarity and therefore special favourites of the radar control points. He had to wait a short while before receiving instructions from the tower, but decided not to let the delay bother him: 'Climb to flight level 70 and report to radio beacon Elba.' When he reached the prescribed altitude, he trimmed the engine and cut the rpms and the flight pressure of the 300-horsepower engine until he maintained a steady flight speed of 200 knots. It would be twenty-five minutes until the next transmission, time enough to listen to the report on meteorological conditions.

Although Marc carried out most of his flights following instrument flight rules independent of

41

weather conditions, it was still vitally important to keep informed about the weather while navigating his little single-engine craft. A bad storm or icing in the clouds could mean disaster, and would at the very least pose some serious problems. For that reason, he liked to be kept up to date on weather conditions.

The last messages he received via the UHF range control of the communications tower had been for the most part satisfactory. At 7,000 feet there was a 500-foot-thick bank of clouds, below which it was raining lightly. At about 18,000 feet there were stratus clouds, and as he flew between the two layers he had a marvellous view. Copenhagen had announced 6/8 stratus clouds a bit lower at 15,000 feet for the route over the east coast of Sweden.

The engine hummed steadily as it carried the plane between carpet and canopy of white fluffy cotton. Marc was reminded of a fairy tale out of his childhood, in which the gates of heaven were reached only after a long procession through the clouds and only those who knew the password were allowed to enter the pearly gates. Whoever was unable to say the magic word had to retrace his journey down to earth. He smiled as he remembered how he had actually trembled for the fabled voyager lest he forget the password and have to turn back. During each flight over the clouds he always asked himself, deep inside, if one actually needed a password to enter into heaven.

He glanced over at Range, who had dozed off. Range believed as much in heaven as in hell, and sometimes he had the notion that Range actually had a password to heaven. To God it might sound silly, but he would probably buy that if the mechanic told him he had the solution. He always had the simplest answers to the most difficult questions, especially when they dealt with God, heaven, hell and life after death. The more success Marc achieved, the more important such questions became to him. But in the end he always pushed them out of his mind, and came back to the view that every man is the master of his own life, and that the solution to life's problems does not lie in the hands of some god but in each man's ability to create a good life for himself.

He glanced down to the left. Directly below them through a small opening in the clouds he could see a patch of trees and a winding river. His thoughts came back down to earth. Once again he occupied himself with the weather. The clouds high above him were becoming thicker and moving closer to the earth. Somewhere up ahead the two layers would converge, perhaps in a cumulonimbus anvil. The temperature was quite warm. Such storm clouds were feared by pilots of even the largest planes, for inside them hail, ice and violent turbulent winds were sometimes hidden. But at the moment he refused to trouble himself with such thoughts.

He switched on the automatic pilot, reported to range control Nora on his altitude and flight time, and went over the Stockholm-Moscow route one more time. According to flight schedule, he should be landing in Stockholm in about an hour's time. There he wanted to refuel and set off as soon as possible on the rest of his flight.

Presently his thoughts wandered back to the matter of the microphone found in his study. Perhaps Dr Ott had brought in the police by now and they had turned up some evidence. It must have been the Russians themselves who wanted to find out something about him in connection with the project, or else others were mixed up in the game. What he could not understand, though, was how someone could get into his own house and the basement of the factory without being observed. And how had his well-protected secret been discovered? He was certain he could not have been betrayed. That was out of the question. Somehow the matter had to be cleared up.

Marc resolved to find out as much as possible during his stay in Russia. Maybe Orlov would be of some help to him.

He glanced over at the wingtips extending out into the milky white of the horizon and noted how they moved up and down with every automatic correction of the course. Just then his navigation instruments showed he had just overflown the Malmö: range control. '... Stockholm control, DENMI here. Am flying over Malmö:, flight level 70 to 45,' he announced. Stockholm took a while to answer, then gave him instructions for landing: 'Clear for descent at FL 50 over Stockholm South. Report to approach control at frequency 179.5 ...' Tasstain confirmed clearance and began his descent.

In the meantime, Range had awakened and was thumbing through the different approach charts taken from the bag between the seats. Then he tuned into the correct frequencies on their radio. During many previous flights together the two had come to function well as a team. Although Range was no pilot, he knew everything a co-pilot ought to know and in Marc's opinion, despite his modest disclaimers, was capable of flying a plane himself.

The radio broke in with their next instructions. Stockholm was having them come down directly, which meant that they would not need to circle about waiting to land. In a few minutes the airfield stretched out below them, and shortly afterwards the Cessna touched down softly on the concrete runway of the Arlanda International Airport.

The next phase of their flight was to take them to Moscow. An hour later, as Tasstain was lifting off the runway in a sharp looping manoeuvre, he knew he would have to traverse a weather front in the Baltic region, something he would have much preferred to avoid. But he deemed it unnecessary to wait in Stockholm for the weather to clear since he had been allocated flight level 150 for his route. At that height he should be able to surmount the storm clouds, but if the information were not quite accurate, he would at most be simply skimming the top of the storm, a situation which was quite bearable.

He left the east coast of Sweden in the direction of Finland around one-thirty p.m. local time and estimated it would take another hour and a half before he reached the coast of Russia, where the bad weather lay in wait. He would then have two-thirds of his flight behind him and a bit less than two more hours to go before reaching his final destination. If everything went smoothly he would even have some fuel left over in the tank for another hour and twenty minutes.

When the plane had climbed to FL 150, they were over the Baltic Sea. The view was so clear that it was hard to imagine that bad weather might lie ahead. The ships and even the ocean's spray were clearly visible. Marc knew very well, though, that this clear view was a sign of the front they were to cross.

Range was busy in the cabin. He climbed in the back and was stowing away their bags and other gear that had been lying around on the seats. It was prudent to have nothing loose in the event of turbulence. Marc fished the large map out of his bag. By recording their position as long as they could see the ground, they would have more of a chance to manoeuvre around the storm in an emergency. He hoped to reach the Russian coast before flying into the cloud bank.

Soon the storm lay in front of them, a huge pile of dirty cotton spread over the land. From outside it looked quite harmless, but when they entered it, the little plane started shaking, as if from fear. Then it plunged and snarled its way through the scraps of cloud till all of a sudden a gust of wind lifted it up into the sky. For twenty minutes this game continued as the plane was tossed hither and thither by contrary winds, and Marc had his hands full keeping on course.

When they reached their next control point, he asked for a new altitude: 'Request clearance for flight level 170.' He was awarded clearance. Taking a quick look at their oxygen meter, he decided that they had a sufficient supply. Soon they began to notice how the turbulence was dying down. All around them it started to get lighter, indicating that they were flying through the top layer of clouds. The temperature gauge fell below freezing. They had to be prepared for ice.

Marc surveyed all parts of the plane that might be the most susceptible to low temperatures. The front portions of the wings were covered with a mist, as if someone had breathed upon them. The danger to the propellers could not be visibly detected, but after a while they were able to discern the somewhat slower movement of the engine. Even the tail of the plane was covered with frost.

It was too soon to turn on the defrost mechanism. The ice was still too thin and would only grow thicker but not be released from the surface. Then it would simply build up more and more, and the defrost mechanism would be rendered useless. Meanwhile, the plane would have lost its manoeuvrability.

The needle of their speedometer continued to drop, as they found themselves flying more slowly. The first effects of the icing were coming into play. The rudders were responding ever so hesitantly. As the ice increased, the craft was becoming dangerously heavy and sluggish. It was high time to switch on the de-icer. A sudden shudder throughout the entire machine told them the ice had been shaken off. In a moment of relief Marc discerned that their speed had returned to normal. However, they were still passing through areas cf turbulence and were being thrown back and forth in the clouds.

He was now in contact with Russian flight control points. The communication was extremely bad, as he had expected. English with a Russian accent was hardly intelligible, especially by radio. They had to guess at what was being said. But Tasstain, the old fox, managed to make headway.

Suddenly the plane was floating like a boat on the water. It had grown dark around them. Range switched on the light, and they both stared into an ominous blackness, which was sure to bode no good. Apparently they were heading directly for the centre of the storm. Why were they not given any alteration in course from the control points below? They must have spotted the storm on their radar and seen that the plane was going to collide with it head-on.

'Mike India, Mike India . . .' The transmitter called insistently in the gloomy stillness. 'Alter your course to 180, immediately ...'

'It's about time,' Marc grumbled to himself, banking the plane in a southerly direction. Then they felt the full impact of the storm, which caught them from behind and tossed them around like a leaf in a March wind. The altimeter went berserk as they were whipped by up and down draughts and buffeted to and fro. It seemed the wings would surely be ripped from the frail craft.

Marc concentrated on keeping the machine under control, as the instrument panel danced before his eyes. At times he scarcely knew which way was up or down, and it required all the skill he possessed to avoid putting undue stress on the controls. Radio contact would have been useless; he hadn't a spare hand. It was all he could do to stay on course.

To his right sat Range, who, though belted in

securely, clung tenaciously to his seat for stability. He uttered not a sound. Never in his life had he experienced such a storm. It comforted him to know that his friend was an expert pilot, able to confront the direst of circumstances. But his composure in the face of danger had a deeper base. He possessed extraordinary faith in God, a faith which never forsook him but gave him strength to cope with any unforeseen fate. He was simply immune to fear. Nobody ever dared joke about his childlike trust.

Tasstain knew of Range's inner reserves from which he had benefited on more than one occasion. Now, in the teeth of the storm, he drew strength from the mechanic's inner tranquillity, and this helped to reduce the tension in the gloomy cockpit. He liked being together with the old man.

Little by little the ferocity of the storm abated. The change in course had been made none too soon. As they flew into a calmer area, the clouds began to part slightly, allowing them an occasional view of the ground beneath. Radar control in Leningrad soon gave them clearance at course 080, which they were to maintain until they reached their destination. The storm had cost them a good half-hour. They still had another hour left before landing in Moscow.

Approaching the capital of this vast country, Marc was increasingly stimulated and intrigued. The landscape had already engaged his interest, but more than that, he found himself intrigued by the people. His first contacts, of course, were by radio. Somehow he found himself transported back to the pioneer days of aviation. Apart from language barriers, he was having difficulty grasping the exact meaning of questions put to him. But the lack of technical skill was more than compensated for by increased personal effort. Marc found that this was the case in all his encounters with this people, whose lifestyle was totally different from that of west Europeans. It was what he most liked about his new undertaking.

Once on the ground, he was met everywhere with unexpected hospitality. But then, he reflected, it was not every day that a private pilot from the West dropped out of the skies into the Moscow airport.

Orlov picked up the two visitors and escorted them to their hotel. He was clearly very pleased. 'The others arrived four hours ago. Did you enjoy your flight?'

'Apart from the weather it was fine, thank you,' Marc answered. 'The storm we encountered is still chilling my bones, but everything else has been a pleasant surprise.'

Orlov smiled. 'You'll soon see,' he observed, 'that Russia also has some truly beautiful weather to offer.'

✦   ✦   ✦

While the others were engaged in serious discussion, Range wandered around through the almost empty lounge of the hotel. It was Saturday, and his time was his own until the following afternoon. At home he had been given the address of a friend with whom he was to make contact. He was supposed to pass on greetings, deliver a package, and find out where he might be able to participate in a mass in German.

He had been advised not to ask at the hotel about how to get to his friend's house, but to make discreet enquiries elsewhere. Perhaps he might ask a taxi driver or just go off on a search alone, as inconspicuously as possible.

Very casually he left the hotel, trying to look as if he had no definite plans. With his hands in his pockets, he meandered by the taxis parked on the street, then, confident no one was observing or following him, went over to the first car, got in next to the driver, and signalled him to drive off. Heaving a sigh of relief, he leaned back without saying a word. At the next intersection he rummaged around in his coat pocket until he found the piece of paper with the address on it and held it in front of the taxi driver. A nod showed him that the driver understood. Through the wide streets they went, past many road junctions until they reached the suburb of the city where the address was to be found.

Range tried to make out the names of the streets they crossed, laboriously comparing the letters on the street sign with the Cyrillic characters on his precious piece of paper. Preferring not to be let out directly in front of the house number, he was gratified when he matched the letters with the name of a wide boulevard they turned into.

'Stoi, platit,' he said in his best Russian. The driver pulled over, and he paid and got out. Looking again at the address on his paper, he made his way to the house and showed it to the old lady who came to the door. He also took out the letter and the package and held them up for her to see.

'Ah, you come from Germany,' he heard her say in a fairly good Swabian dialect. Without waiting for his answer, she opened the door and invited him in.

Range was glad he could at last speak German to someone, and during the conversation he discovered that the young people were out of town visiting and the grandmother was taking care of the house in their absence. They were of German descent and, though they had lived in Russia for many generations, they had preserved their language and customs. Range listened to the old lady as she described Russia as she knew it. The Germans had never really been accepted and had always had to cope with difficulties. New obstacles were constantly thrown in their path. The only thing that kept up their spirits, apart from the unity that existed among them, was their devotion to the German church.

In the course of the conversation, Range found that a mass was to be held the following day. The lady explained that it was no ordinary religious service, since everything had to be conducted in strict secrecy. She told Range that the Russian authorities would often seek out and arrest church leaders so he must not mention the service to anyone. Her son, who returned later that evening, arranged to pick him up near the hotel the next day.

As he travelled back to the hotel on the bus Range felt pleased that he had been able to carry out his errand so quickly and he was delighted that his wish to attend a religious service was to be granted.

☆　☆　☆

Following their lengthy talks with their Russian hosts, Tasstain and his colleagues went on a tour of the city of Moscow. The primary attraction was Red Square and the Kremlin, that grim, high-walled citadel with its cathedrals and palaces crowned with gold and silver domes and cupolas. As they continued their tour, the group were allowed to stop occasionally and view some of the sights on foot. Finally, full of new impressions and tired out, they returned to the hotel in time for dinner.

Tasstain lay on his bed unable to fall asleep. Once again his thoughts would not leave him in peace. Despite the fact that he was marking up one success after another in his profession, was financially well off, and had a happy marriage, he felt restless and unfulfilled. What was it that was missing? The project with Russia – his project – seemed to be taking shape and was an enterprise that certainly added lustre to his career in the machine factory. Still he was not happy. Whenever he left home and felt a bit lonely, questions would start swimming in his head. What was true happiness? Wealth, independence, achievement? All these he possessed, yet still he was unsatisfied.

Travel to distant lands offered a pleasant diversion and business trips sparked new energy, but always some inner longing would gnaw at his heart, taking the edge off his enjoyment. He would set off in his plane for some remote destination, hoping that there he would find an answer to his indefinable yearnings, yet no sooner had he arrived than some force from within would urge him on, so that he found himself in an endless quest for fulfilment. Some day, he kept telling himself, he would find what his spirit longed for. Perhaps it would happen in this singular land ....

He rolled over on his other side. Suddenly there was a knock at his door. 'It's me, Range. I just wanted to tell you I was back.'

Tasstain got up and opened the door. 'What are you doing up so late? And where have you been?'

'I was visiting friends of some acquaintances in Germany. By the way, they've invited me to attend a religious service tomorrow afternoon. Would you like to come along? It's supposed to be something special and ought to prove pretty interesting.'

Tasstain considered a moment, then accepted. This was a chance for him to forget his brooding.

'Don't say anything about it to anyone,' cautioned Range, 'because it could cause trouble to the congregation here.'

'All right.' Tasstain promised to keep quiet and said goodnight to the old man. A little while later he at last fell into a deep sleep.

The next day the two men found themselves being led on a roundabout route to an old brickyard outside the city where the German service was to be held. Only someone familiar with the area could find this deserted spot. On the way, Range explained to his friend the special circumstances under which these parishioners came together.

'They're not allowed to practise their religion, since almost any type of genuine religious activity is forbidden here. Beyond that, they are ethnic Germans, whose lives are made difficult anyway. Since the leadership of the country is atheistic, any Christian activities are labelled counter-revolutionary, at least when they are not under the control of the authorities.'

When they arrived Tasstain quickly decided that he was not looking at any gathering of counter-revolutionaries. The entire congregation was made up of modest, rather shy-looking people, who scarcely seemed capable of any uprising. The two strangers were welcomed warmly, with everyone wanting to shake their hands. The isolated group could not hold back the joy that spread among them at the sight of visitors from Germany.

The mass itself was different from anything Tasstain had ever experienced before. A number of men took it in turns to stand behind an improvised pulpit, open up their Bibles and read a few verses. Each offered a few words of comment on the text, in a way unfamiliar to Tasstain. It was as if people from another world were staging a play before him, and he was carried away by it all. How could human beings in such difficult circumstances radiate such confidence? Most of them were probably very poor and employed in tedious work. He saw this in their hands, their dress, their movements. But in spite of a nearly hopeless situation, they seemed to be genuinely happy. Had they perhaps found what he had been searching for?

The event lasted almost three hours and went from

preaching to hymn singing. Then there was a performance by the children. From time to time spontaneous prayers were offered. Some people were in tears, but it was evidently no sad crying, but rather tears of joy. Again and again the name of Jesus Christ appeared in the prayers, as the Saviour of mankind, the Deliverer from all evils, the One who brought peace on earth. Tasstain recognised one of the songs they were singing: 'I pray to the power of love.' Yes, it had to be genuine love that had taken hold of these people. He was aware that something deeply moving was taking place here.

Glancing at Range, he observed that the old man belonged to these people and possessed the same aura of certainty and confidence. He found himself wishing that he too could be one of them, one of these happy people.

While the congregation was singing the last verse of one of the songs, the black-bearded Sorvas slipped unnoticed into the brickyard and cast a swift glance over the gathering. Precautions always had to be taken, for now and again outsiders and spies would sneak unawares into the congregation. He immediately spotted the two strangers, and finding himself unobserved, withdrew to one of the rooms nearby. He planned to wait there for the elders, who were supposed to get together after the mass for a short meeting. If his presence had not had a specific purpose, he would have preferred to disappear. However, he was in search of some men he could trust to help him clear the garage of the paper from the warehouse. The Stranger had given him the exact hour at which the paper should be removed, and he wanted the operation to proceed smoothly.

'Who are those two strangers?' Sorvas asked the elders as they greeted one another.

'They are friends from Germany,' the man who had

driven them from the hotel replied. 'They are here with a delegation that is in charge of the construction of a factory.'

'Have you all gone berserk?' Sorvas hissed. 'Such people are constantly under surveillance. Don't be surprised if you're not all put under surveillance before long.' Afraid that his whole paper-removal scheme was in jeopardy, he refused to stay any longer in the brickyard. As soon as he had been promised a couple of men for the next evening, and been assured that they would take an oath of complete silence, he disappeared as inconspicuously as he had arrived.

Tasstain and Range, who stood waiting outside the half-open door to the small room, could hardly avoid overhearing the conversation. Although the arrangements made no sense to them they felt the tension which lay in the air. Little did they realise that they would soon be dramatically involved in the lives of these people.

☆   ☆   ☆

Whoever believed that the Russian secret police knew nothing about the work of the clandestine parishes was only fooling himself. They had a fairly good idea which parishes existed and even knew about their publications, although often they were not sure where the printed matter was coming from.

Major Tukov, head of the department in charge of 'underground work', was going through a list of all the forbidden writings and their dates of publication. The material was categorised according to the degree of danger posed by its contents. It would have been virtually impossible for Tukov to prevent the publication of such material, but there was a great deal he could do to limit its spread. Most of the originators were familiar to him and had only to be arrested. But it was of more importance to obtain a list of the recipients. With such a list he could wipe out the entire political and religious opposition in the underground.

Curiously, it was not Tukov's job to prevent the material from leaving the country. In fact, it was even to the government's advantage that the world should know of the existence of an opposition movement. It would encourage public opinion in the West to believe that the system was not all bad. Furthermore, citizens of the free world would have their crusading zeal dampened by the thought that an active underground, be it ever so weak, was also functioning.

Consequently, Tukov merely limited the amount of dissident literature allowed to pass into foreign hands. This KGB agent was feared even by his own bosses, who knew only that he had some of the best contacts. Whoever opposed him would sooner or later disappear from the scene, naturally without any proof of complicity.

It was not without difficulty that Tukov managed to let the information get to the West. The border patrols were so well organised that he had to outwit his own comrades – no simple exercise. On the one hand this material had to appear as if it were being smuggled out of the country, while on the other hand he had to ensure that if it were uncovered the operation could not be traced back to his office. This extremely complicated double game that Tukov masterminded had led to his connections with top party officials. In his personal struggle for power, he had thus been able to further his career. This work also brought him into contact with Western authorities and gave him limited authority to issue passports and visas.

What Tukov now had in front of him was not an ordinary dissident letter. It was a list of two hundred detained Christians from various unregistered churches, accompanied by photographs, dates of arrest, location of detention, and in some cases other data regarding age or family.

The question confronting him was whether he should allow this information to leak into the West. For him it represented the highest degree of risk. From past experience he knew enough not to expect any drastic reaction from the free world, though religious organisations might protest mildly. But Tukov had his people strategically placed so that he could make sure not too much dust would be stirred up. Since he knew it was possible for this information to leak out through other channels that could prove much more detrimental, he decided to pass it on at the next opportunity.

And it was not long before he had devised a plan. Learning that a delegation of German businessmen was in Moscow on an official visit, he got in touch immediately with the Ministry of Economy. 'Comrade Orlov, I hear that you are in charge of a German delegation. Have these people already arrived?'

'Yes, yesterday as a matter of fact, Comrade Major. But what's this got to do with you?'

'Only a routine affair. Would it be possible for one of us to join in the tour of the city? We will hardly be noticed at all.'

'Of course it would, but I'd like to call your attention to the fact that we are dealing with an important company and that no disturbances are to be allowed,' Orlov warned the Major, somewhat perturbed that this impenetrable fox should get himself mixed up in the affair.

'Everything's okay, Comrade. As usual we'll go unnoticed.' Tukov hung up the phone, reflecting that it was better that this was a top priority delegation. It would save him some trouble.

* * *

Piles of wood lined the road taken by the black limousine on its way to the paper factory. It looked as if all the forests of Russia had been collected to impress the visitors. At the entrance to the factory stood the director, waiting to bid them welcome. One of Tukov's men was also on the scene. Like the engineers on the technical staff, he was wearing a blue construction hat, pretending to be what he most assuredly was not. After everyone had shaken hands, he worked his way over to Tasstain in order to find out more about the project. During their visit to the factory, he constantly engaged Tasstain in harmless conversation, using all his expertise as a spy. He specifically wanted to know how the pilot had been controlled when he arrived in the country by plane and where he had left it. He urged Tasstain to come to him for help should he need any technical assistance.

Tasstain, who was grateful for the unexpected offer, naturally had no notion why this friendly man was asking so many questions. He seemed honestly interested in the German's welfare and spoke freely, without that constant note of distrust that Tasstain soon discovered was part of the ambience of the country. He overcame his usual reserve and, throwing caution aside, found himself chatting freely with this man.

And so the agent was able to obtain all the information he needed to smuggle the papers into the plane and out of the country. The only concern was how to avoid the routine controls of airport security, but that was a minor problem in view of Tukov's power. At any rate, the plan was to be carried out a few hours before take-off.

At first glance, the paper factory looked like a very well-organised enterprise. However, Tasstain was quick to observe that this state was not normal. The premises were old and by Western standards of scarcely any use. But of course one would not measure by the same standards. Human labour was cheaper in this country and the demand for quality lower.

As he toured the factory and stood to watch the men at work, he was met with a variety of expressions, some mildly curious, others almost frightening in their intense distrust. Under such circumstances, it was natural for him to try to bridge the gap with a friendly smile. Sensing the penetrating look of someone behind him, he turned around to encounter the attentive eyes of a black-beared man who was in the process of unloading paper. Where had he seen him before, and who exactly was he?

Before Tasstain could nod his head in greeting, Sorvas turned away to lift another box. He had recognised Tasstain immediately. If someone were to notice that they were not meeting one another for the first time, there could be dire consequences.

Sorvas had learned that the German had arrived in a sports plane and now the black-bearded man was pondering a new scheme. Why not arrange for Kovlenko to leave the country with Tasstain? A plane would not have to go through any border controls. If Kovlenko could be brought to the plane secretly and if the pilot agreed to the plan, it had to work.

Sorvas racked his brains to think of a way to contact the German. Then, like a bolt from the blue, the idea came to him. Quickly he scribbled down on a scrap of paper torn from the rolls the words: 'Sunday, same religious service. A friend from the church.' He crumpled up the paper and as inconspicuously as possible trailed the group of visitors who had entered the transport depot. While Tasstain was standing a little to one side, Sorvas slipped the message into his hand, moved casually on, and disappeared into another room.

Now he was totally in the power of the foreigner. If he were betrayed by the German, inadvertently or otherwise, he was lost. But Sorvas knew that such an opportunity would not come again, and time was running out.

☆　☆　☆

Back in the hotel, Range brooded over the message from the black-bearded man. 'Did you see that man in the congregation?' he asked Tasstain, who had just come in the door.

'I can't remember exactly, but he must be connected somehow, otherwise he wouldn't have picked that place to meet.'

'It could also be a trap. Maybe someone saw us last Sunday and wants to find out more.' Worried, Range thought about the extraordinary measures taken to ·conceal these meetings and the strict penalties that faced those in charge.

'I'm inclined to think that there's something urgent that forced the man into taking that step,' Tasstain responded, attempting to turn the old man away from his gloomy thoughts. 'He hardly even knows who I am and is willing to risk more than we are. No, we'll go there another time. I'm starting to get interested.'

The following Sunday the abandoned brickyard once again filled up with people, who risked arrest week after week because they belonged to an illegal

German congregation, lived out their commitment to Christ, exercised freedom of religion, and shared their beliefs with others. They were always on guard because they worshipped their God and not the State with all its violence. Though they were among the hardest-working and most conscientious of citizens, they were looked upon as outcasts. But nothing could keep them from following the words of God and practising their religion.

On this particular Sunday hundreds had come to the mass – young and old, a lively, heterogeneous crowd, who showed no sign of dismay at the dismal situation they were in. Tasstain had already been strangely attracted to these people. Somehow he felt good among them, sensing their independence from the world in which they found themselves and admiring their determination to swim against the current instead of capitulating to it. He liked the fact that these people resisted the oppressive actions of the government though there was no hope of success. They were held by a spiritual bond that provided them with the strength they needed.

Some of those present greeted the visitors. Many were already aware of the reason for their visit and were delighted at the contact with their father-land.

Now Sorvas pressed through the crowd to Tasstain. 'May God be with you, stranger!' The sounds rumbled through his beard as he extended a powerful hand and almost crushed the Geman's. Two pairs of eyes met, held briefly, and gave approval. Everything was clear. No prejudice existed between these two men.

Sorvas pulled Tasstain through the crowd into a quiet corner of the room. 'We don't have much time, and this is a matter of the highest importance. You've probably noticed what's going on in this parish. But such independence isn't tolerated without government or army officials in the leadership who can observe everything very carefully and report it to their superiors. Since the country is officially atheistic, that keeps a congregation from growing, and it's not the kind of religious life we want to lead. We don't want to work against the government, but we just want freedom to plan for ourselves in our religious undertakings. And we want to know for sure there are no enemies within our flock.

'Our position naturally has its consequences. Many of our leaders have been arrested on some pretext and brought to court on charges of treason. They usually receive sentences of several years' imprisonment in jail or detention in camps. Countless numbers of our elders have been disposed of in this way and end up spending the best of their years in prison under barbaric conditions. Since our Christian belief does not permit us to use violence, our only alternative is to flee or hide.

'In order to bring about a change in our situation, we try to inform the West about the hopeless conditions of Christian groups and to convey to them the misery of our broken families. But, as you doubtless know, no one is allowed to leave the country without permission from the authorities. And that's why we need your help.

'One of us must escape to the West, whatever the cost. We can get hold of neither passports nor permission to travel abroad, and therefore only illegal routes are left open to us. And because I saw you here....' Sorvas found it difficult to put into words what he wanted to say. 'That is, since you won't have to pass any border controls with your plane, I thought maybe you could take one of us with you.'

Excited and anxious at the same time, the black-bearded man fastened his eyes on Tasstain. If Tasstain had an inkling of understanding, then surely he would be willing to attempt the risk. But looking at

Tasstain's worried face Sorvas began to suffer pangs of doubt. Had he said too much? Had he overestimated the foreigner?

Meanwhile Tasstain was churning inside. Yes, he had imagined himself helping someone in distress. He had asked himself how he might be able to help the congregation attain the freedom it so desired. But those had been fantasies, a mere play of thoughts. Now that he was directly confronted with the problem, he felt confused, apprehensive. He longed to refuse on the spot. Such an undertaking was out and out dangerous. He would be jeopardising his firm's entire project. If this affair were uncovered, how could he ever face Orlov again? There was no limit to the consequences if things went wrong. Even if they refused to fire him, management would still have to remove him from this project. That could mean the end of his entire career.

He thought of his wife Dora and the children. They too would have to pay the consequences. Then he remembered the microphone in his study. Someone had already spied on him and knew where he was. Was someone laying a trap for him? A myriad thoughts hammered at his head. Then he heard himself saying, as if in a dream, 'Right, I'm willing to take someone along. I don't actually know how or even if it will work, but I'll give it a try.'

Sorvas's face lit up. In his delight he longed to hug Tasstain, but he restrained himself. Now, at least, everything could be planned. The first step was to find the right people to carry out the mission.

He pulled out of his pocket a folded sketch of the Moscow airport. 'It's best if the man doesn't get in the plane until shortly before take-off. That would be the easiest solution, even though it will be very difficult to get him into the airport terminal unnoticed.'

'Hmm, to the hangars – I don't really like that idea.

The risk of being caught is too great. Isn't there a possibility that, say within a hundred-mile radius of the airport, I could land and take someone on board?' Tasstain had seen many empty fields and meadows while flying into Moscow, and he knew his plane was suitable for landings on such rough terrain.

Sorvas considered the idea. He hadn't thought of this possibility, since he was unaware of the plane's capabilities. 'Of course there is,' he concluded. 'About sixty miles west of the city there's a valley. On both sides there are flat open meadows, which would certainly allow you to land and take off with no problems. There's a village nearby, but it's far enough away to pose no hazard – about eight miles. I could have Kovlenko brought there. Right near there we used to hold youth meetings. I know the area like my own neighbourhood.'

This suggestion Tasstain liked much better. The risk could at least be calculated. Airport security and routine controls would by then be safely out of the way.

'A few minutes after leaving I could be at the meeting point. Everything has to go like clockwork. Wait at the end of the field in the direction against the wind. Place a red or white cloth to mark the spot.' He got Sorvas to describe the area to him once more, and he memorised all the details, especially a description of the end of the field where the river bends and leads into the forest. He then promised to inform Sorvas of the date and time of his departure.

The mass had already started. Suddenly it grew silent. All eyes were fixed on the leader of the gathering, who stood Bible in hand behind the improvised pulpit. 'In the name of the Father, Son, and Holy Ghost, amen. Our help be with God, who created heaven and earth.' The words of the preacher rang out clearly above the heads of the silent congregation, when suddenly a sharp command shattered the stillness.

'Everyone stay where you are! The building is surrounded! Those who resist will be shot!' Three army soldiers stood at the entrance with their machine guns pointed at the gathering. It was obvious they meant business. Through the window openings shadows could be seen scurrying around the premises. Outside, trucks ground to a halt, and soon the tramp of boots resounded throughout the building, as it was given a thorough search. Commands were shouted. Dogs barked.

Paralysed and frightened, the Christians watched as the sudden tornado of action whirled around them. When the soldiers turned towards the pulpit, the people started to come alive. Like a melting bank of snow, they surged into the wide passageway in the middle of the hall to cut off the soldiers' access to the pulpit and moved around their leaders to protect them, but the situation was hopeless. In the face of brute force they were as defenceless as a flock of sheep awaiting the slaughter. It took only a short while for the worshippers to be shoved violently into the trucks. Once again an illegal religious service had been uncovered and broken up.

What happened was nothing new. Many such gatherings had been disrupted in this manner, even those that were not so clandestine. Those who were taken off always knew what was in store for them: incessant hearings that would end with the arrest of those in charge. Sometimes, bystanders arbitrarily caught in the raid were also detained – a tactic used to intimidate the public.   Tasstain and Range were among those seized. The soldiers pushed and pulled Tasstain viciously as he started to protest. It did him no good to attempt to explain that he was merely a tourist. He gave up the useless struggle and followed

Range, who patiently awaited destiny's call. Sooner or later the authorities would discover that a mistake had been made in arresting the two, and Tasstain would demand an explanation.

Sorvas was fortunate in that he was able to escape without being seen. He had not hesitated for a moment when he heard the soldiers. He was a veteran of many such experiences and knew what his arrest might mean. Before the officials had been able to assess the scene, he jumped down a hole in the floor leading into the cellar of the brickyard and made his escape to safety through an exit outside the building. He at least was able to outsmart the bloodhounds. Meanwhile, those who remained were taken off by truck to the hearings.

☆   ☆   ☆

On Sunday night Orlov waited in vain for Tasstain. The two of them had arranged to go to the theatre together and had agreed to meet in the hotel lobby. Puzzled and impatient, he called the hall porter. 'Ring Mr Tasstain's room and try to get hold of him.'

'Mr Tasstain was seen going out this morning and hasn't returned yet.'

'Was he alone?'

'No, Mr Range was with him. He hasn't returned either.'

Orlov looked the man straight in the eye and asked, 'Is it known where the two went?'

The answer was hardly audible: 'Unfortunately not; our man lost his trail. The only thing we know is that they were heading for some church, but we don't know which.'

Orlov rushed to the telephone. He knew very little about church goings-on but was sure he knew who might be able to help him. 'Comrade Tukov, you know our visitors from Germany. Two of these men went to some church this morning and haven't returned as yet. I'm worried about them, because we were supposed to meet tonight and no one has turned up.'

'What happened to your tail?' was the prompt rejoinder.

'That's exactly what's troubling me. He was given the slip. And I don't want any scandal over this. You know the visitors are to enjoy VIP treatment, but we have to do something. If I only knew which church they'd gone to! Could you help at all?'

'Of course I can tell you where a church is, but how would that help matters? Maybe they've made contact with other Germans. There are religious communities among the Germans, but most of them are forbidden. But if they wanted to attend one of those services, it would explain why they needed to lose the tail.'

'But they couldn't have known they were being tailed. They had no reason whatsoever to believe they were being followed.'

'Probably they'd been warned by members of the church. Like as not those people invited them somewhere after their service and they forgot all about meeting you. I'd wait until tomorrow morning. No doubt the two will have returned by then.'

Orlov hung up the phone reflectively. The affair didn't please him at all, but perhaps Tukov was right. He could wait until tomorrow.

☆　☆　☆

As Tasstain was thrown into the cell and the bars clanged shut behind him, everything exploded in his head. Never before had he been robbed of his freedom, and it was especially difficult under such circumstances. As a foreigner, he couldn't make himself understood, and he was not able to talk to Range, who had apparently been placed in a different cell. The entire group had been herded into the cellar of the court building where some were put into solitary cells, others in groups. All he had been able to find out was that it would be some time before they were questioned. He might even be one of the last, and then it was questionable whether they would even try to believe him.

His only hope was that Orlov would get word of his detention. By the next day at the latest he would have noticed that the two had not returned to the hotel. But would he discover where they had been taken? Who would tell him that they had attended an illegal religious service, and who would believe they had been thrown in jail? All the members of the congregation had been arrested, and it was apparent that this action was being kept secret. Not a single soul would find out about it, not even the other departments. Then how in the world was Orlov to find them?

He had noticed that Sorvas suddenly disappeared in the brickyard, but where to? What would happen if the authorities found out about the planned escape? He could well imagine that in this place it would not be too difficult for them to make even a man like Sorvas talk.

The memory of his brother Mike flashed into his mind. What brutality had the secret service used years ago to wipe out seventy lives merely in order to dispose of him! What would keep these people from committing further gruesome crimes? The fate of his brother was so real, so close to him. He saw clearly how cold-bloodedly these people were dealt with and how futile it was even to try to defend oneself. The congregation, too, was fighting a hopeless battle against the will of the state. How dearly they paid for meagre results. As he was about to sink into despair, he heard the sound of soft singing. In the cell next to his, the prisoners had started singing: 'Almighty God, we praise thy name. Lord, we praise thy strength. The earth bows down to thee and is in awe of thy works. As it was in the beginning, is now, and ever shall be, amen.'

Tasstain could hardly believe his ears. Here they were sitting in prison with a brutal hearing and perhaps many years of imprisonment awaiting them and they were singing a song of praise! Wasn't it this strong and almighty God who had brought such suffering upon them? Where was this wonderful might? Where was this bowing down? His mind in a turmoil, he lay down on his cot and tried to sleep. What would Dora think of his predicament? And oh, the children!

☆   ☆   ☆

When Orlov entered the hotel the next morning and still found no trace of Tasstain, he called up Bugitchkov and told him about the disappearance.

'Today the final talks were to take place, and the crucial person isn't here. I can't believe that Tasstain would forget this appointment. Something must have happened. What should we do? You probably know that Tukov has entered this affair. First, I thought he might be responsible and last night I gave him a ring. He thought the two probably went to a German religious service and got delayed.'

'To a German service, you say? Yesterday an entire congregation was broken up.'

'What do you mean, broken up?'

'I only got word that an illegal gathering had taken

place which was broken up because no permission had been issued. I haven't been informed of anything else. In this case, they were German by descent. That's why I thought of the incident.'

'At least that tells us where we can begin our search,' Orlov sighed. 'Thank you.' He hurried to his car and drove to the police station. He would not be able to get any official information, since such matters were kept secret. But he knew if he talked with the right person he might be able to glean some news.

Meanwhile, Tasstain found himself being interrogated. Two close-set eyes under a mean brow examined him narrowly. 'Didn't you know,' the officer roared in fluent German, 'that this gathering was forbidden?'

'No,' Tasstain answered and then tried to explain who he was.

The officer cut him off. 'Oh,' he said sarcastically, 'you didn't know that approval was necessary for such meetings? Who did you go in hiding to meet?'

'Now, listen here...'

'Shut your mouth and speak when you're spoken to!' the officer hissed. 'Name?'

'Tasstain.'

'Age?'

'Forty-three.'

'Country of birth?'

'Germany.'

'Place of residence?'

'Germany.'

'I asked where you lived. Don't smart alec me!'

'I live in Germany and am here only temporarily. Furthermore, I shall report you...'

Before he could get any further, the officer hit him across the face. 'It seems to me you've forgotten that you were picked up at an illegal, subversive meeting and have to pay the consequences. It doesn't matter to me whether you've been here a few days or a thousand years. It's my duty to find out who is acting against our country and going against the law.'

Tasstain's face turned to stone. Never in his life had he been so humiliated. He felt he was about to lose control of himself. With every beat of his heart a new wave of anger engulfed him and overwhelmed any rationality he might possess. In one movement he grabbed the officer by the front of his uniform and dragged him across the table.

'Who gave you the right to hit me, a foreigner, across the face?' he burst out. Then he slammed the astonished officer up against the wall, knocking him motionless to the floor. Panting, Tasstain bent over him as the door was forced open and two military soldiers barged into the room. He raised his arms to try to protect himself, then lost consciousness.

☆   ☆   ☆

Orlov stood next to Tasstain's bed in Moscow's prison hospital, shocked at what he was seeing. It had cost him a lot of trouble and much talking before he was able to have Tasstain released from his cell and transferred to the hospital. Now he gazed at this stranger with his head totally covered with bandages who stared back with vacant eyes. At a loss for words, Orlov tried to start a conversation.

'I simply cannot understand how something like this could have happened!'

Tasstain remained silent.

'Why didn't you ask for me, or at least mention my name? Or better still, inform me of your plans in advance? Unfortunately there are many restrictions in our country that may seem strange to you.'

'Restrictions?' With a great deal of effort Tasstain tried to sit up. 'These people were horribly beaten.

71

Those aren't restrictions, that's pure brutality. It's incomprehensible to me how such a wise man as yourself could believe that the use of such violence could prevent opposition. Better citizens than those humble, hard-working people a state could hardly wish for, but instead of supporting them, it tries to oppress them. The core seems to be somewhat rotten, my dear Orlov.' Exhausted, he lay back down. 'What happened to me isn't important. I should have controlled myself and waited for you. But those Christians – what should they do? Are they to give up their beliefs, which give them energy and the will to live? That's the best way to destroy someone's will.'

Orlov sat down on the edge of the bed. 'The state is not concerned with brutally beating anyone, but with trying to prevent the spread of a religion that's closely related to capitalism. You know how much injustice has been perpetrated in the name of Christianity. Hasn't the Christian state proved time and time again that it can't solve its problems, either with religion or violence? Why then shouldn't our non-Christian state be given a chance to try?'

'... and make the same mistakes?' Tasstain thought out loud. 'Beatings and secret detention are medieval methods for which you killed the czars of Russia, and now you do things that are ten times worse. And don't forget to make a distinction between Christian belief and a Christian state. Christian states have many times been guilty of indefensible activities throughout the centuries. But how much worse are the crimes of your Comnunist state! How many of these believers are now in detention? Your country used to be very religious. Yesterday's incident only serves to prove that millions have met the same fate. Oh, no! You'll get no sympathy for such methods....'

Observing how exhausted Tasstain was, Orlov remained silent for a while. Then he got up to go.

'As soon as you're on the mend, I'll personally bring you back to your hotel. Meanwhile Mr Range can visit you any time. Our final talks have been postponed for another few days. Sleep well, and forget what happened. Think of the project – there's still so much work to be done.'

A bit unsure of himself and put out by arguments he couldn't meet, Orlov left the hospital room. Tasstain, tired and drained by the conversation, told himself before falling asleep that he had made the right decision when he promised to help Sorvas smuggle Kovlenko out of the country. These brave people had to be given more than moral support, even if it meant encountering more trouble ahead.

☆　☆　☆

Silvia Schmitz sat in the midst of a number of pictures she had taken of the factory in the last three weeks. Her cheerfulness and unaffected manner as a waitress in the factory's canteen had enabled her to open many doors, literally as well as figuratively. She had access to the workshops, the factory halls, and even the design offices, and no one had the slightest notion that this handsome young lady might be involved in something evil. She always greeted everyone with a friendly hello and seemed able to anticipate a need before it was expressed, providing coffee and sandwiches just when they were required.

Even Dr Ott, the confirmed bachelor, came to like her and talked with her as often as occasion allowed. This puzzling young lady seemed to have endless interests, and he enjoyed more and more being able to answer any questions she might pose.

The fruit of her labours had been plentiful. In addition to photographs of nearly all the technical installations, designs, calculations, and documents, her file was bulging with details on all the company's products and machines, together with exact information on the running of the factory, and personal data on the families of the employees. Since the information on the absent Tasstain was not yet complete, she could not conclude her mission. She had not risked asking questions about Tasstain in the factory since the microphone she had planted in his house had malfunctioned. This had led her to conclude that it must have been discovered. But Ott seemed more and more anxious to get into conversation with her, and she hoped to receive from him the last bits of information on Tasstain, the key figure in the factory.

Meticulously slipping the photographs one by one into a hidden slit in the wallpaper, she complimented herself that this hoard would not be dug up very easily. Then she disappeared into the ladies' room.

Tonight she was having dinner with Dr Ott. Although she knew her work would be in peril if she allowed herself to follow her heart, she cherished the prospect of being with him. The cool, level-headed, lanky intellectual had done that to her.

'I'm glad we could be together,' he said, offering her his hand somewhat awkwardly. 'If you have no objections, I thought we could go to a Chinese restaurant. What do you think?'

'Oh, that's fine with me. I like foreign food a lot better than German anyway, and besides, there'll be a certain oriental magic about it.'

'Are you very familiar with oriental magic?'

'No, no,' she said in a hurry. 'I've only come across it in books and films, and somehow it fascinates me.' Actually, she had already been in the Far East, spoke beautiful Japanese, and had been assigned on a mission in Japan as a specialist in industrial espionage. But as a waitress in a canteen she could hardly talk about that. Ott himself had long since come to the conclusion that she did not fit the job, but presumed there had been some misfortune in her personal life and chose not to ask questions. He was more and more attracted to her and felt quite at ease in her presence. But he was an academic, more at home with books than with people, and this had kept him from revealing his feelings to her.

The conversation did not follow the course the attractive agent had originally intended. Both were enjoying their meal and found themselves gazing into each other's eyes for longer periods than a first date really warranted. Each was deep in thought, she planning her game of harmless questions, and he wondering how he might get her to talk about herself. It was not very often that Dr Ott invited a lady out to dinner, and easy conversation did not come naturally to him. In truth, he had taken her to his heart and felt no great need to talk. It sufficed that they were together.

'I see you a lot with that older man who always eats in the canteen,' the agent ventured. 'Has he left the factory?'

'You must mean Range. He's abroad on a trip with Mr Tasstain. They'll be coming back soon – with news of success, I hope.' Ott became talkative. 'Then this trip could prove very important for the company. We're all very anxious to hear all about the delegation's experiences, especially the part concerning our factory. Whole departments were working on it, and I don't know how many conferences were held. Besides, we miss Tasstain round here. He's virtually indispensable, and Range is what you might call the mother of the bunch.'

'You seem to like them both a lot.'

'Well, truthfully, I guess I do. We get along

marvellously and work closely with one another on...oh, different developments.' He almost let something slip about the printing machine but apparently his faltering stutter went unnoticed.

'I hardly ever see Mr Tasstain around,' she added, casually. 'He really seems to be an important person. But tell me a little about yourself,' she said with a smile, trying to lure him away from the topic she most wanted to discuss. She saw that Ott was again falling out of his talkative mood and decided it was still too early for specific questions about Tasstain.

'My life up to now has been pretty monotonous. After my studies and practical experience, I was a professor at the Univesity of Gottingen. But that got boring and I decided to try my luck in industry. For many years now I've been with the same outfit. That's the whole story! But I do feel good when I can calculate and develop, read and reason, and now that I've made so many good friends here I've become a fixture. Nobody'll prise me loose.'

'Oh, I'm totally different. If I stay in one place too long, I get restless and have to have a change of scenery. I couldn't bear living without change. Of course, that could be due to the fact that I have no roots and only myself to take care of.' Her voice had a tinge of melancholy, which was not lost on Dr Ott. He seized the occasion to follow up on it.

'Would you prefer to live for someone else?' He was anxious to hear her reply.

'Well, living alone has its advantages and good points, but something is missing if you can't share your feelings and life with someone else. I think experiencing something alone is only half as beautiful as sharing it, don't you think so?'

'Yes, you could be right,' he added thoughtfully. 'I was thinking more about being there for someone, being at someone else's beck and call, gearing one's own life to that of another person. Of course, sharing experiences is part of that, but it seems to me a person's existence becomes quite circumscribed. The word *victim* isn't exactly what I mean, but somehow it suggests being tied down to someone else.' That fear of losing his independence was what had kept him from getting involved. He hated giving up his own life, his own interests and desires.

'I believe this willingness or ability to share comes with true love,' she replied, smiling, and he thought he detected an ironic sparkle in Silvia's eyes as she said this. But she had automatically laid her hand on his, and her warmth and affection passed easily into his innermost being.

Later, while driving Silvia home, he found himself lost in thought, with new feelings surging inside him. For the first time in his life he felt a bond, an urge to open himself up to another person, an attraction he was helpless to resist.

Silvia, on the other hand, was plagued with a rare case of bad conscience as she observed Ott's growing fondness for her and realised that things were taking a serious turn. What kind of human being was she? Could she never be truly sincere? Didn't it matter to her that she was just pretending to like someone in order to extract the information she needed? Why did she have to be in this dishonest occupation, from which there was never any turning back? For this man, she realised with a pang, she would have been willing to start anew....

Then, in disgust at her own weakness, she tossed away her scruples. Wasn't it a man, after all, who had ruined her life and robbed her of all her dreams? Anyway, her present job matched her abilities and gave her a sense of satisfaction. Ott could only play a role in her game, not in her life. She decided to finish her job as quickly as possible, pass on all her information, and get involved in a new task in order to forget Dr Ott.

☆ ☆ ☆

Before his departure for that perilous rendezvous in a small meadow pinpointed in unknown terrain, Tasstain would have dearly loved to speak once more with Sorvas. But if he were to show up in the hotel, it would only jeopardise the whole plan. Contemplating each stage of the rash plan, Tasstain saw many weak spots that could lead to failure. The crucial moment was undoubtedly the illegal landing. If it were detected, retaliatory measures would immediately be taken to thwart such a subversive act. In the eastern border area it was not unusual for planes to be forced to land, even when they had only strayed off course and been unaware they were flying over foreign – and therefore illegal – territory.

The only real protection for the mission was the absolute secrecy that had been maintained, not to mention the priority granted Tasstain for the flight, especially after his mix-up with the secret police. Orlov was doing his best to protect him from any more trouble. That meant not letting him out of sight. Either Orlov himself kept an eye on him or he was surrounded by amiable colleagues from the Ministry of Economy, who attempted to satisfy his every wish. He was treated like a king, taken everywhere he wanted, but he was not alone for one minute during his last days in Moscow.

It was the black-bearded Sorvas who made the arrangements. After he had managed to escape from the brickyard, and while Bugitchkov's bloodhounds were busy questioning and removing the congregation, he had a long talk with the Stranger, outlining the details of the planned escape on the German plane, and asking for advice.

'We really ought to talk to the pilot one more time,' Sorvas commented, 'but that's literally impossible since he is constantly in the company of members of the Ministry of Economy. We were only able to talk very briefly about the landing and we have to rely on his memory when it comes to locating the field near a bend in the river about sixty miles west of the city. The plane is supposed to land there about thirty minutes after leaving Moscow and take Kovlenko on board. We had no map, and I couldn't remember the name of the village that lies eight miles away.'

'Couldn't we somehow get a map to him with the details?'

Sorvas scratched his head. 'I think that would be too risky. Even if we were able to hand it to him directly, someone is sure to be watching. And Tasstain doesn't know how to react in such situations.'

'What did you say the man's name was?'

'Tasstain. Why?'

'How old would you make him out to be?'

'I'd say fortyish.'

'Do you by any chance know his first name?'

'As far as I can remember he was registered in the list of visitors to the paper factory with the initial "M".' Sorvas was puzzled by the question. The Stranger turned around and fidgeted about at his desk. Then for a long time he remained silent, staring out into space. Suddenly, with a look of determination, he pulled out a map and unfolded it.

'I'll pass this on to him in a way that no one will notice,' he said crisply. 'For we have to be absolutely positive about the meeting place. Beyond that, we need to know the exact departure time, unless we want to risk everything. By the way, I want to be present during the landing.'

Sorvas lifted his brow. 'You really want to be

present? Isn't that a bit unwise? If something should go haywire, they'd suspect a lot more if you were found there. That could mean dire consequences for all of us.'

'Leave that to me. I know my way around perfectly. And I also know how we must act. When we're certain we're at the right spot, everything will go smoothly and no one will be any the wiser. As soon as I know more, I'll get in touch with you. Then you'll have to be ready to leave within two hours. We'll drive separately to the rendezvous.'

On the map they marked the bend in the river and the green meadow and memorised the way to get there. Then they separated.

Sorvas had never seen the Stranger quite so agitated. The affair seemed to preoccupy him beyond measure. But for the moment he was more concerned with his own state of mind. Never had he needed such steady nerves for a mission. But there was no reason to believe something would go wrong, he reassured himself, as he set off to find Kovlenko and instruct him of the plan. The old man had to be prepared to move quickly as soon as the departure time was set.

☆ ☆ ☆

Marc was packing. He would have preferred to stay around for another few days, just to postpone the forthcoming flight. His mind was in a whirl, with all sorts of misgivings. It seemed impossible that they could pull off the mission. He threw his things into his case, at once irritated and apprehensive. Again and again he tried to picture all eventualities. What would happen if Moscow Airport called him during his descent? Within a certain radius around Moscow he had to maintain radio contact, and for a certain distance he could still be detected on the radar screen. He could only pray the landing site lay beyond. The quicker he got off the ground again the better, he decided.

He opened a drawer, looking for personal belongings, as his mind raced on. Radio transmitters could also malfunction every once in a while, without sending a jet hastening in pursuit. And after all, emergency landings were not forbidden – were they – if some engine problem arose? Only how to find the field – that was what worried him. How many similar fields might there be?

A knock came at the door. It was Range. He also had to be let in on the plans. The ever-cheerful man bent over and picked up an envelope that had been shoved underneath the door.

'Another message for you,' he said.

Marc examined the envelope carefully. *Tasstain* was all that had been written on the front. He tore it open and took out a map, on which a red dot had been marked. Clearly it was at the bend in the river where the landing was to take place. On the map someone had scribbled the words 'Please leave time of departure in hotel room'. He gave a whistle of relief and slapped Range on the shoulder.

'Co-pilot Range, what would you think of an emergency landing in the middle of Russia?'

Range looked horrified, put his finger to his mouth signalling Marc to keep still, and pointed to the ceiling. Had he lost all his senses to speak about such a thing in the hotel, even if in jest? He had to know they were being bugged.

'I'm not too keen on the idea. But why should something like that happen to us here? We've never had to make an emergency landing before.' He tried to undo the error, and fortunately Tasstain caught on immediately.

'I was only kidding. Of course we'll make it home without any mishaps. How's your packing going? We want to be off after breakfast.'

'I'm all ready and set to go. I can't wait to be home.' As Range left the room, Marc stuck the map in his flight bag. That was a close shave, he thought. He had almost bungled the entire mission.

Following breakfast, when they returned to their rooms for their luggage, Marc slipped a piece of paper on the bedside table with the departure time, eleven o'clock. There was nothing more for him to do. It was only a matter of waiting for the final countdown. Soon they would find out if the undertaking were a success.

An hour later, after a cordial farewell from Orlov and his colleagues, the two Germans finally climbed into the cockpit. Range stowed away their gear and then held the checklist on his lap, reading off item after item while Marc tested the instruments, switches, and safety devices. 'Fuel...both tanks full....' The clock showed ten-forty. They had already filed their flight plan and were waiting for runway clearance.

The airport was relatively small, for all its importance as the port of entry to the vast country's capital, and its runways were easy to follow. The airport crew seemed exceptionally vigilant, making sure that the plane took off smoothly. Soon they received clearance on runway 24, with take-off from 'Alpha Charly'. In front of them a four-engine Tupolev stirred up the dust, obscuring their view. They could follow the radio messages between the control tower and the huge plane, and as the big bird lumbered off the ground, they received their confirmation of schedule.

'Delta Echo November Mike India, you are cleared

for VFR flight to Stockholm via runway 24...radio beacon South...VOR...POD...route 3...flight level 40. Report flight over POD. Over.'

Marc repeated the instructions, then rolled on to the runway, adjusted his electric compass to 240 degrees, and shoved the throttle forward. With the engine at full speed, the plane lunged down the long runway, and after a couple of short hops, like a waterbird leaving the surface of a lake, it leaped into the air. Soon the craft hung in the milky grey sky over Moscow. Its two occupants exchanged glances, then drew a sigh of momentary relief. Behind them, hidden beneath one of the back seats, was a package containing Major Tukov's confidential papers.

Range took a look at the map on which the landing point had been marked. They were flying south. Route 3, which they were supposed to use, led them twenty miles north of their meeting place. After they had diverted from their course it would take seven minutes to reach the field and land. Before this, Tasstain had to report to range control Podolsk. There they would leave behind them their departure frequency and – they trusted – the radar screen of departure control, and report to Molensk information. But Marc hoped to be able to postpone making this transfer until they had completed their landing.

Now they were flying over the departure beacon South and took up course for the next beacon POD. Meanwhile they had reached 4,000 feet, with moderate visibility. White mist prevented them from having a clear view of the ground, though they could still see the dark forest areas below. Only after leaving their departure control frequency, after passing over range beacon Podolsk, would Marc be able to descend from this altitude and search for the landing field. He had to approach the meadow directly, since circling around too low would not only cost time but arouse the curiosity of nearby residents. He decided he would rather take a short detour over a river flowing from the east that would lead them to their destination. That meant, he calculated, that immediately after his last report he would have to head east, quickly leave his altitude, then find the tiny river and follow it to the point where it joined the Moskva. From there it was three miles up-river to the bend where the field was located. He would fly over the meadow twice to assess the terrain and check for obstacles before risking a landing.

Just then the needle of his UHF dial indicated that they were over VOR Podolsk, and Marc reported his position. As expected, he was asked to change frequencies. 'Contact Molensk, information on 119.50' came over the loudspeaker in stumbling English, eliciting a heartfelt, 'Thank heavens!'. He switched on the new frequency without reporting in, charted an easterly course, and began his descent, sinking 200 feet per minute. Soon he would have a better view of the ground. He pulled back on the throttle as they gained speed. Both Marc and Range scanned the terrain for the small river. In a few minutes they were down to 2,000 feet, bringing the mountains and valleys ever closer as the horizon shrank. At 1,000 feet they could clearly make out houses and roads.

'There it is!' Range exclaimed. They descended even lower, to where they were engulfed in the valley. To the right was a crest of hills, to the left a road following the line of the river. The plane soared through the valley, dipping its wingtips like a bird as it followed the windings of the ribbon of blue.

Now the convergence of the rivers lay ahead, plainly visible as the clear stream mingled with the muddy water of the Moskva. Marc pulled the plane sharply to the right, following the river upstream in a southwesterly direction. Six minutes had already elapsed. The visibility worsened because of the ground fog blanketing the Moskva valley. On the one hand the fog was welcome, since they could not be seen. But it was only an added obstacle to finding the meadow.

The high-wing craft flew smoothly over the middle of the river at about 100 yards. Both men concentrated hard on their projected course, looking for the bend in the river. Marc cut out the throttle with a sweaty hand and lowered the nose so as not to lose sight of the banks. Out of the mist appeared a high row of poplars, behind which the river-bend shimmered. He guided the plane to the right – and there it lay, a long, wide stretch of green – their landing field.

From the air it looked like a plush green carpet, but as they inspected the field more carefully, Marc noticed a fence cutting across it, shortening his runway considerably. The only possible way to land was in the direction of the river bank with its poplars, but the tail wind would be an added hazard.

Flying over the meadow, Marc could see no piece of cloth nor any people. Once again he banked sharply to the right to take a better look at the fence, then turned for the final approach. As slowly as possible, with flaps down and engine throttled, he attempted a landing. The chosen field looked smaller and smaller as he approached, propelled by a slight tailwind towards the ever larger poplars. Nose high, they sank over the fence and the wheels finally touched the ground.

Marc had virtually no control over the light machine, which at landing speed bounced and lurched over the rough terrain towards the bank of the river. He applied the brakes but noticed immediately that the grass was wet and the plane slipped sideways. He let up on the brake, then pumped it gently until they reached a patch that had been mowed, enabling them to come to a halt a few yards from the poplars and the muddy river.

'Whew!' Marc heaved a sigh of relief as he dismissed the momentary vision of a crash in the trees. Range buttoned the top button on his shirt, ran both hands over his hair, and ventured, 'At least we're in a perfect position for take-off.' He knew enough about flying to realise that a tailwind can be deadly, whereas taking off into a headwind would give them added lift with their heavy load. But they were not ready yet to think about lift-off. There had been no cloth marker, and there was no one in sight. And time was running out.

Range emerged from the plane, stretched momentarily, and scouted the area in all directions. Marc sat nervously in the cockpit tapping his fingers on the steering mechanism. They would not be able to wait very long. If some stranger turned up they would be obliged to leave, for their own safety. Maybe they had been seen or heard by local residents who even now were on their way to investigate the strange visitor.

Searching his map to see if by any chance they had made a mistake, Marc convinced himself once more that they were at the agreed spot. He decided to wait another ten minutes before continuing. Longer than that and he would risk everything. He knew that if they remained off the frequency too long someone would start looking for them. Range trudged around the machine and opened up the baggage compartment from outside.

'Might as well get everything ready so we can get out of here in a hurry,' he said, confident as ever. 'They're sure to be here in a couple of minutes.'

A car suddenly appeared at the other end of the field and came jolting towards them, crossing the rough ground with some difficulty. Behind was a second car. It had to be them.

'Thank heavens,' Marc sighed with relief – but then he was struck with a sudden doubt. Why two cars? 'Let's wait and see who gets out.'

'Oh, nonsense,' Range said. 'Who else would be getting out? It'll be the black-bearded one and Kovlenko and friends.'

Marc stared expectantly as the cars drew up alongside the plane and stopped. The first man to get out was unfamiliar to him – or was he? It wasn't possible ....

'Mike,' he gasped, scrambling awkwardly out of the plane, nearly falling in his haste. His long-lost brother stood before him, and clear-eyed. The two brothers stared at each other for a long moment, then fell into each other's arms. While the rest of the group stood around in some confusion, Marc, completely over-whelmed, drew back and looked his brother up and down, holding tight to his shoulders as if he could not believe this 'stranger' actually was his own brother. Mike was almost a head shorter than Marc, slim and fine-boned. His sharply cut face and steel-blue eyes radiated a cool confidence.

'I had a notion it might be you after hearing Sorvas mention your name.'

'But Mike, what happened to you? Where have you been? Why have we never heard anything from you?'

'Too many questions all at once, which I can't answer right now. We've already been talking too long. You must continue on. Don't speak to anyone – and that goes for all of you,' he added, turning to the others. 'And on no account must you write. I'll get in contact with you.'

Although Marc knew they had no more time, he could hardly tear himself away from his brother, who had appeared as if from the dead. It was his deepest dream come true. As all these thoughts crowded in and his emotions ran high, he was on the verge of forgetting the dangerous mission he was on. But

Kovlenko brought him back to reality. Taking him by the arm, he reminded him that they must be off.

'You have taken on a very difficult task, which is only just starting. I understand how difficult it must be for you to leave, but we have to.'

Sorvas, too, was urging haste. He was more touched by the scene than anyone might have sensed. As the brothers embraced each other in farewell, tears came to their eyes. How small the world was, after all. How great was God's goodness – and how little man understood.

Range had long since stowed away the baggage. All that was left was to get aboard, which Marc did with mixed feelings. He started his engine, cast his brother one last long glance, and headed the plane into the wind, bumping and bouncing over the rough ground towards the fence. The plane with its extra load lifted off just in time and headed toward its previous bearings. The detour had taken thirty-five minutes. During this time they had been out of radio contact.

'Delta Echo November Mike India, here is Molensk information speaking at frequency 119.25. Please report.'

'Here DENMI. How do you read me?'

'We read you 4. Give us your position and altitude.'

Although Marc had not yet reached the prescribed height, he reported in at 4,000 feet with position forty miles west of range control Podolsk. Granted he would only reach this position in another twenty minutes, but he hoped no one would notice where he really was.

'What happened, DENMI? We lost you. Is something wrong?'

'Everything's okay. My transmitter wasn't functioning properly. You didn't answer my calls.' To make it sound more credible, he let go of the speaking key a couple of times while talking, so that his message was not received clearly. They accepted his excuse.

'Mike India, report fly over beacon Riga, and maintain your altitude.'

Marc repeated the command, then leaned back and relaxed. Now he could breathe more easily. The next report was not due for thirty minutes.

As he relaxed, a sudden pang of joy shot through his being as he thought of Mike. The totally unexpected reunion with his long-lost brother now took on a quality of remoteness, of a dream half-remembered on waking. He deliberately blinked his eyes a couple of times and squeezed the controls to reassure himself that the events of the past weeks and the strange circumstances leading to the brief encounter had not been one long dream.

A glance at Range jerked him back to the present, and Kovlenko's presence behind him told him it was all real.

In an alien land one sunny day, in a green meadow by a muddy river, his lost brother had emerged like an apparition and had embraced him. The thought was overwhelming.

What had taken place in the lost years? He could scarcely imagine. His brother's reappearance was as mysterious as his disappearance. How he ached to know more! The encounter was so brief, so – unreal. He wondered if he would ever hear from his brother again.

Kovlenko, sensing Marc's turmoil, laid a hand on his shoulder. 'I thank you for what you have done,' he said quietly. He grasped the significance of the incident in a way that Marc, for the moment, could not. He also knew that under normal circumstances the brothers would have taken much more time, but the extraordinary nature of the venture on his, Kovlenko's, behalf made that impossible. He was aware of the risk Marc was taking and of his great personal sacrifice.

Kovlenko lapsed into deep silence. He felt the need to pray for this man, as he always did when he came close to men and their destiny. Prayer had long since become a way of life for the old man. During his many years of detention he had not only learned to work but to pray. And because his outlook was positive, he was able to survive his years in the camps of Siberia. He had been sucked into the Gulag because of his belief, but because of this belief he was alive. Anyone who knew him sensed that, however weak and helpless he might outwardly appear, this man had a deep spiritual strength. His confidence and security came from a God who was not ruled by chance and coincidence but was working out his own plan for the salvation of mankind. Kovlenko believed strongly in guidance and obedience and hoped that Tasstain would come to that same revelation.

Meanwhile, Range was nurturing much the same thoughts, and so it was that two men, high above the clouds on that fateful day, said a prayer for Marc that was to have far-reaching consequences.

☆   ☆   ☆

Before the Cessna had crossed the German border and long before its final landing on the home field, Silvia Schmitz knew what her next mission was to be: supplying the German press with certain sensitive information. Just as she was contemplating how she could best carry out the job, Dr Ott walked into the canteen holding a piece of paper.

'In four hours they'll be landing,' he said with none of his usual calm.

'Who?' Silvia asked.

'Well, who else? Tasstain and Range, of course. You know – the visitors to Russia.'

'Oh, of course. Then all went well, I presume?'

'I've only just received word from Stockholm about their estimated time of arrival. That's all I know right now.'

'Well, then, you still have time for some Irish coffee.' She smiled and disappeared into the kitchen. Ott went over to the canteen phone and gave Dora Tasstain a ring to tell her the good news.

'I'll have a car sent over in plenty of time to pick you up and take you to the airport .... Of course, you're happy .... Naturally, I can understand .... See you later....'

Silvia brought him a cup of hot coffee with a good shot of whisky. As she set it down in front of him, Ott regarded her out of the corner of his eye. She was really very attractive and radiated from her somewhat ordinary appearance a unique charm. For a long time now he had been wanting to speak to her quite frankly but had not mustered the courage to do so.

The hot coffee warmed him and melted his inhibitions. 'Come here and sit next to me. There's no work to do right now, anyway.'

Silvia pulled her chair over next to his. She had to admit to herself that she enjoyed his invitation. 'Do you have time? The last few days you practically disappeared. You didn't come in here even once. I thought maybe you'd caught a cold or something.'

'You know,' Ott said, ignoring her question, 'I've been thinking about the two of us. It might sound dramatic, but I had to be clear about my feelings for you, and I wondered what you thought of me.' He felt awkward, but at least he had got it off his chest. Maybe the Irish coffee had helped.

Silvia was momentarily speechless. She had never expected such candour from Dr Ott. But at the same time she was overcome with a warm, contented feeling. In actual fact, she realised she had longed for such a conversation. In spite of her professional reserve, Ott had occupied her thoughts for a long time.

Her amazement sounded sincere. 'My feelings toward you? What am I to say?' Ott saw that for the first time she was a bit unsure of herself. But she regained her composure very quickly. 'You know I like being with you and don't enjoy talking with anyone else as much as I do with you. But I have to admit I haven't allowed myself to have deeper feelings.'

'But I have. I had to, because I couldn't get you off my mind. Please don't be offended. Such things have to be discussed and brought out into the open, don't you think so?'

'Oh, of course. In fact, I think it's very important for us to share our thoughts openly. I feel it's better to be straightforward, even if,' she said softly, looking away from him, 'it's not always possible.' She raised her eyes and met his gaze as if she wanted to give him some sort of sign that there would always be an unconquerable barrier between them.

'And now let me get some more Irish coffee, since we almost have a reason to celebrate. The return of your flyers from Russia would be reason enough, not to mention your confession.' It almost sounded a bit sarcastic. She jumped up to fetch the drinks from the kitchen.

When she returned, Ott looked at the mug, then turned and courageously took her hand in his. 'Up to now I've always written down my thoughts. I note the pros and cons of a particular woman and usually come to the conclusion that I should remain alone. With you I've broken the rule for the first time, and that has made me think seriously.'

'Oh,' she said brightly, 'does that mean I have only advantages to offer?'

'No, no, that's not it. I didn't even start keeping an account because I guess I didn't want to see any disadvantages in you.' He warmed his hands on the coffee mug. 'Please tell me, do I cause a similar reaction in you, or do I leave you completely cold?'

Again Silvia was taken aback. She was in such an awkward position that she even started to stutter. 'No of course not, absolutely not – I mean – that is, you don't leave me cold or indifferent, dear Dr Ott. I'm very fond of you and would also like to talk with you about it, but you'll have to give me time.' Now she had taken hold of herself again. 'And now, think about your friends who will be arriving soon. They'll surely have a lot to tell. And don't forget to pick up Mrs Tasstain.'

Dr Ott, shaken out of his dreams, had no time to be disappointed. He had completely forgotten! Hastily he finished his coffee, promised to spend more time with her next time, and set off for the airfield.

☆ ☆ ☆

Tasstain set down a bit hard on the bumpy runway of his home field. One could tell the plane was heavily loaded. Slowly, almost wearily, it rolled over the field to the apron, where Dora Tasstain and Dr Ott were already standing.

Stiff from the last leg of the flight, Tasstain got out first, followed by Wilhelm Range. Finally, they helped an old man out of the craft. During their half-way landing in Stockholm, Kovlenko had remained hidden on board so that no customs controls had been necessary. Here on this little airfield, all the customs officials knew Marc well and didn't even ask for his passport. They never suspected that he would be bringing in an illegal person. So Tasstain was able to smuggle Kovlenko in without causing any commotion and without needing to announce where he was from.

Marc walked straight over to his wife and cupped her face in his hands. 'You were alone such a long time, Dora. Everything went well, thank heavens!' She smiled at him with a contented look and said nothing.

'Yes, it's God we have to thank,' said Kovlenko gently, as he stood behind them with folded hands. All at once, as if it were the expected thing to do, everyone turned and gathered around him with bowed heads, as he invoked heaven in a brief, glorious prayer of thanks.

Then Marc insisted that they get on their way. He most certainly didn't want to run the risk of having inquisitive spectators ask tricky questions. In the car he introduced Kovlenko to everyone and gave only the briefest explanation of why he was there.

'Then Mr Kovlenko will be staying with us for a while,' Dora announced. She liked this old man who had been bold enough to attempt such a daring escape and was glad to have the opportunity to make her own contribution, however insignificant.

Marc was content. So far everything had gone well. Now they had to achieve their next goal – publicising the affair. He intended to inform the press as soon as possible and to make the necessary arrangements for Kovlenko to present his information to the public. Dr Ott would probably be the best man for this job.

☆ ☆ ☆

When Dr Ott got out of his car in front of the press building, he practically knew the story by heart. After Tasstain had filled him in on all the details of the trip, harrowing as well as rewarding, Ott, far from being his cool, dispassionate self, was actually eager to become involved. The next day he was on his way to the newspaper office. Grasping his briefcase containing typescripts of the information that Kovlenko had brought in, he shut the car door and stepped off the kerb to cross the street. Just then he spied Silvia coming out of the press building.

'Hello!' he called, half glad, half surprised at the unexpected encounter. Silvia stopped in her tracks and glanced in his direction, unsure of what to do next. Ott zigzagged across the street, jumping behind this car and avoiding that truck, till he reached the other side.

'What are you doing around here, young lady?' he queried, trying to sound witty.

'Oh, nothing special. I've just placed an ad in the paper, and now I'm looking for someone to go to lunch with,' she replied with a jaunty air. 'Are you game?'

'And how! I just have to run a quick errand, then I'll be ready. Wait across the street at Bolsi's for me. We can have some of their special crêpes. Women who look for men to go to lunch with must be particularly hungry,' he added, as he escorted her to the pedestrian crossing with his arm around her in a gesture of friendship. 'See you in a few minutes, you voracious thing!' He turned and was soon lost in the crowd of people.

In his delight at the thought of having lunch with Silvia, he lost a little of his enthusiasm for his present assignment. As quickly as he could, he reported to the news editor. There he was amazed when the short, stocky gentleman, after glancing through his sheaf of documents, threw them down on the table with the words, 'Hey! What you've just given me someone else brought in just half an hour ago. To tell you the truth, this has never happened before with such unique papers – though I've gone through quite a lot here, believe me.'

Ott looked at the documents, then at the editor. He was plainly puzzled. 'That certainly is strange, and a complete mystery to me. Who brought you those documents, may I ask?'

'You'll laugh – a pretty young lady. She told me she couldn't say much about the papers. Had merely been ordered to drop them off with the request that they be published. She said that the contents would speak for themselves.'

'A young lady?' Ott asked. 'You couldn't describe her, could you?'

'Around thirty-five, dark,' was the prompt answer. 'She looked a bit severe, but very pretty.' The editor smiled. 'At any rate, she didn't quite fit in with the affairs these papers apparently deal with.'

'The information is, of course, very important,' he went on thoughtfully. Then he straightened up, determined to deal matter-of-factly with the subject. 'It concerns scandalous facts which, as you no doubt realise, ought to make a good story on a hot issue.'

'In our newspaper we only cover current issues. At least, that's what everyone believes who has something to report.' The stocky little man thumbed through the stack of papers with an obvious lack of enthusiasm, then studied one sheet a bit closer and read aloud: 'Andrey Ostapenko, born October 27, 1935, arrested on March 11 for participation in a mass held in a forest, sentenced to 10 years forced labour, 11 children, the five eldest having been delivered to a state reform school.' He leafed further through the papers: 'Vladimir Biblenko, 65 years old, the oldest in the congregation, was taken away for questioning on November 14 and brought back a few days later in a coffin, having allegedly suffered a heart attack. As the family insisted on opening the coffin, they discovered Biblenko had been beaten to death.' In the attached photograph there was the horrible picture of a maimed corpse.

The editor continued to thumb through the documents. 'It seems to be the same story more or less throughout the entire pile!'

'You're right. Whoever reads all that just can't keep silent any more. Will you publish it?'

'I believe we can make a report on it, but we have to be careful. The public doesn't want to read too much about such hideous things. How did you happen on these documents?'

In a couple of sentences Ott summarised the factory's project and the delegation's visit to Russia. 'But it wouldn't be advisable to mention the name of this company in public. The project is being sponsored by the government, and they definitely want it to be implemented as – shall we say – a showpiece for further economic cooperation.'

'I'll see how we can manage. It would be better to join this information into a story. But I'm not the only one to make this decision. If I have any questions I'll give you a call.'

'Good! And you might let me know if anything on it will be printed in the paper. Thanks!'

In a hurry to go to lunch, Ott bounded down the stairs. At Bolsi the main rush had already subsided. At the entrance he pushed his way through the lunchtime traffic coming out of the restaurant, then scanned the place carefully. It was a huge room with a large window. The tables, beautifully decorated with floral arrangements, were set in little niches. He caught sight of Silvia sitting behind one of the tables.

The sunshine streamed through the leaves of a palm and illuminated her face, painting it with light and shadow. The severity of her fine features was accentuated magnificently. A serious-looking but pretty young lady of about thirty-five! Ott moved towards her quickly. She must be the one who had brought the documents to the editor before he did. The scales fell from his eyes. Yes, she must have had something to do with the entire Russian affair. That seemed perfectly clear. But what role did she play in it?

As he greeted her he was caught up in a whirlpool of thoughts. Where had she been able to get hold of this information at practically the same time he did, and what was her interest in seeing it published in the newspaper?

Silvia gave him a sunny smile. Apparently she was happy to have bumped into him, and she bubbled over with joy. 'I've already eaten one crêpe. I was waiting for the second one till you arrived. They taste best with curry or mango chutney.'

Ott tore himself away from his thoughts. 'Okay, make it two curry crêpes and an ice cold beer.'

Turning to Silvia, he tried to be his usual self. But she couldn't help feeling she was being examined somewhat critically, and it made her uncomfortable.

'Is there something wrong with me?' she asked, in an attempt to clear the air.

'Oh, no, everything's fine.'

She couldn't possibly know he had just come from the newspaper with the same assignment as hers, he mused. But why had she not mentioned anything? Why the lie about the advertisement? Ott ate his crêpe in silence. Something didn't add up – in fact, he was sure he smelled rottenness somewhere. But he was so fond of the girl that he kept the matter to himself. He was unwilling to get her into any trouble, and so for the moment he kept quiet. He knew he would have to find out more. Perhaps the entire matter would turn out to be a mistake, or maybe there was a simple explanation for it.

'So, tell me about your announcement. What kind of ad was it?'

Silvia stopped eating, then slowly wiped the corner of her mouth with her napkin and looked at him in surprise. Her eyes didn't flicker as she turned on him her practised mischievous smile.

'You're pretty curious, aren't you, my dear? Is that so important to you?'

'Not at all!' he said hastily. 'Just such a strange coincidence that we should meet in front of the newspaper office.'

'Yes, that's true. What did you have to do there, by the way?' She adroitly turned the focus off herself.

'We've received documents from Russia on the inhuman, authoritative measures used by the government against Christian minorities. That's what I took to the paper to have published. The injustice described is unimaginable and intolerable. We hope that by publishing it we can help the people involved.'

The mischievous look on Silvia's face vanished. Caught completely off guard, she momentarily lost her usual quick-wittedness. It was only because of her long years of experience and her special education that her brain continued to function and search for a credible explanation to give Ott. If he had submitted such documents, then he also knew that someone before him had done the same and apparently he presumed she was the one.

There was only one thing for her to do: acknowledge an affiliation with Russia and in so doing pretend she was a fighter for human rights, or else say she had been given orders by someone to deliver the papers. Then she had the urge to confide in Ott and tell him the true story. After all, she knew him so well that she might be able to risk it. Hadn't she often contemplated putting an end to her double existence? To her snooping in others' affairs? To the constant danger of being discovered and the stress of always having to be a jump ahead of her 'victims' in order to make her escape?

She was well aware of the risk she would be taking, especially since she was a conspirator in many secret plots. No doubt her contacts would try to dispose of her. But for once, for the first time really, she saw in Dr Ott her one true chance to escape from the vicious circle of agent activity. She was sure this was the moment when she would have to wager everything she had. Laying her hand upon Ott's she said, with the utmost seriousness and candour, 'I want to confess a secret to you, my secret – and it will not be easy for you to accept.'

☆ ☆ ☆

Since Kovlenko had entered the Tasstain household, life for them had changed. Dora and the children often gathered around the old man listening to him as he told in his broken German about Russia. His collection of stories was inexhaustible. Everything he had experienced and his way of recounting the details were all so exciting that the family were enthralled and could hardly get enough. What made his tales so special was the way he interpreted his experiences for himself and others.

'If a man believes in God and doesn't hide it from others, then he belongs to the soldiers of God,' he explained to the oldest Tasstain child. 'As a soldier, he can count'on a battle, knowing that if he doesn't fight he cannot win. This is no ordinary struggle, such as one faces in sports, or business, or politics. This is a struggle that, in the last analysis, deals with life in its essence. A life without God is empty and renders everything worthless. With God, on the other hand, life has meaning and value. And purpose,' he added, thinking of his own past. In spite of his many years in prison, he could honestly say he had lost nothing, but rather had gained a different kind of wealth, peculiar to those who have undergone such experiences.

'How do you believe in God?' the fourteen-year-old wanted to know.

'First of all, you have to hear and read about him,' the old man said. And so from that time on, the Bible was read regularly in the Tasstain home.

Marc was very happy about it. Kovlenko had provided answers to many of his own questions too. For this reason, he was one of the most avid participants in the nightly discussions with Kovlenko.

One night, just as the family were all getting up from the table, the telephone rang.

'Mr Tasstain? This is Ott. I have to see you right away. Could you come over to the company directly? Range is here too. We'll be expecting you in the basement workshop. This is a very important matter that has to be dealt with immediately.'

When Marc entered the room where the new printing machine was also located, Ott and Range were waiting for him expectantly – but not alone. Silvia Schmitz was with them, looking apprehensive, like a small animal afraid of its new owner.

'What on earth is going on?' Marc exclaimed, looking from one to the other. 'I confess I'm completely in the dark. Here's a stranger in this room, and you two sit as though it doesn't matter.'

'That's how I felt too,' Range said, 'until I found out what was going on. Go ahead, Ott, tell him. He should be quite astonished.'

And so Ott told him the story, bit by bit, exactly as Silvia had related it to him, starting with the first delegation of Russians, the detailed preparations of the Soviet secret service, the surveillance of all the employees of the firm, and the almost complete photographic material on the production machinery. To top it off, he concluded with her thorough description accompanied by film documentation of the new printing machine, which was to be tested in the near future.

It took a while before Tasstain grasped the full significance of these details. His first reaction was to acknowledge to himself that his initial premonitions had been justified. Far worse was the realisation that the entire operation had been part of a perfect scheme, with everything planned to the last detail. He shuddered. Here was industrial espionage and outright deceit carried out to perfection by a government itself, at what level he could only imagine. It had all been prearranged that at the right time the Russians would call a halt to partnership and continue the project on their own. But outwardly everything had its specific order – talks, negotiations, contracts used only to avoid investment costs. At a certain point the parent company would have no further influence whatsover. The Soviets had cleverly, and with a friendly smile, stolen all the expertise and experience of one of Germany's soundest enterprises.

Momentarily stunned, Tasstain felt anger welling up within him. 'And you allow this...this...person to sit around here?' he spluttered. 'Shouldn't the German secret service have been notified by now, or at least government authorities been called in?'

Silvia's heart throbbed uncontrollably and her mouth went dry. Dr Ott swallowed nervously. Range stepped into the breach.

'Here lies our real problem – or perhaps our chance. Of course, we can call an alarm and let the whole affair blow up. But that wouldn't stop the Russians from continuing with their plans. As a matter of fact, it would probably spur them on to break off negotiations and carry on without us.'

'And the machine?'

'They'd silently cash in on that, on the side. Then nothing would be known about it, not even to anyone here.'

Ott cleared his throat, carefully preparing to speak. 'Let me remind you that Silvia Schmitz has voluntarily laid all her cards on the table. She has, as far as I can see, told us everything from A to Z, which means she herself is in the greatest danger as soon as the Russians find out we know everything. For several reasons, I believe we should go on as if nothing has happened.'

'What, stand by and watch the game, and see the Soviets drain us of everything, while they go unpunished?'

'No, not at all. Miss Schmitz is on our side now and can help us find a solution....'

'Ott, how can you be sure of her intentions? Haven't you ever heard of double agents?'

Silvia got up. 'Mr Tasstain, I can understand how you must feel right now, and I realise you have no reason to believe me. At the moment I cannot prove anything to you but I would like to convince you of my sincerity. The step I took, Dr Ott is responsible for. I trust him. Believe me, I am not only in your power, but my life in is your hands – and theirs, if they happen to find out. I wouldn't be worth tuppence to them, then. If I'd continued with them, you'd have gained nothing. Now there is a slight chance that we can mislead them for a while, which will give us time to consider how we should handle the affair.'

Tasstain's indignation subsided to the point of allowing him to say, though with an edge of irritation, 'Okay, let's leave it for a while the way it stands. Tomorrow at the same time we'll meet here again to discuss the matter further. Dr Ott, you're to be responsible for this Miss Schmitz, or whatever her real name might be. And you, Range, close up here as usual.

'Goodnight!'

☆   ☆   ☆

The following day in different newspapers a sensational story appeared about the perilous life of Christian minorities in the Soviet Union, where an underground church movement was struggling against great odds to keep the faith alive. Some news reports asked if German churches had done all they could to make others aware of the drastic circumstances of these people, since the general public had practically no idea that persecution of Christians even existed in Communist countries.

At first the article had the impact of a bomb. Countless phone calls to the newspapers proved that the public was aroused and interested. Many were astonished, horrified, furious and above all willing to help in any way they could.

But while they expressed positive interest, the authorities on the other hand were unwilling to take positive action. The reaction of the churches was totally unexpected and, indeed, unaccountable. Articles appeared warning against sensationalism, and religious commentators decried uncritical acceptance of the alleged 'facts.' They said that the reports were doubtless highly exaggerated and furthermore were not official since church authorities knew of no instance of oppression nor the name of a single persecuted Christian. There was no mention of sympathy for the suffering or concern for their plight.

The KGB plan was right on target. On the one hand,

the report implied that in a totalitarian state there was organised opposition to oppression, making foreign intervention unnecessary. On the other hand, the churches, which people turned to for further information, reacted by pouring cold water on the documentary value of the report, rendering it ineffective. Because of the euphoria over detente, politicians were willing to overlook evidence of injustice, even though the press disclosed new sensations.

Nothing would have come of the whole affair if it had not been for the presence of Kovlenko, who, with the help of Tasstain's connections, wrote letter after letter, published circulars, phoned politicians, and spoke before members of the press. As a result of his impassioned activities, a group of people organised a committee to grant regular assistance to Sorvas and his parish.

Meanwhile, Tasstain himself was far from idle. To save the project and his invention, he came up with a dangerous but ingenious plan. He intended to recover all the material handed over to the Soviets. Naturally, this would only be possible with the help of Silvia Schmitz and his brother Mike.

Night after night Marc, Ott, Range, and Silvia met in the basement of the factory to discuss every last detail of the plan. The first task was to get in touch with Mike Tasstain. That was Silvia's job. She was scheduled to go to Russia anyway to hand in her next report and could then make contact with Sorvas and 'the Stranger', arranging for the material to be taken near the Finnish border at a given time. Tasstain would fly there and pick it up.

The most difficult part of the scheme was the procurement of the material. According to Silvia, Orlov kept it in his office and was waiting for day 'X' to use it. Since she was under orders to work for Orlov's ministry she was able to come and go as she pleased and with a bit of luck and expertise might be able to sneak out the file.

The transport from Moscow to the border was simpler but might also engender some surprises. This part of the plan would be up to Sorvas and Mike. The flight over the border between Russia and Finland was no less tricky. Marc had to fly beneath radar range, remain unnoticed, and determine in which forest area around the border the most suitable landing site was to be found.

Dr Ott was glum. 'That'll never come off. There are too many difficulties.' Besides that, he feared for Silvia. Range scratched his head. A lot could go haywire. Marc turned to Silvia and eyed her narrowly. 'And you, what do you have to say?'

'You know, in the life of an agent such a plan is nothing new. Our jobs aren't your everyday run of the mill sort – but they can be fatal. We have a real chance that this will succeed. It will all hinge on how carefully we lay our plans. And since this whole mission is virtually in my hands and I am dependent on very few people, I say let's take the risk and dare it.'

Marc relaxed. 'Good! The sooner the better. Tomorrow we'll talk about the details. In a week the plan has to be ready.' As soon as their course of action had been worked out, he wanted to talk it over with Dora and Kovlenko.

☆   ☆   ☆

Preparations for construction of the factory in Russia were finally completed, only awaiting the signal to start from Orlov's ministry. Orlov himself sat in his office sorting out construction plans, contracts, and all the other details of the operation. Bugitchkov had brought him the last stack of files. It was marked

'Confidential' and contained all the information on the factory in Germany which had been gathered by the KGB department for industrial espionage.

From the package Orlov removed an envelope containing photographs. They showed Tasstain's printing machine: clear, exact shots of all the parts of the machine. Gradually Orlov came to realise that this must be a sensational new development, an electronic wonder. The machine acoustically recorded a text and transmitted this information to the printed page. In other words, one could speak into the machine and wait for the message to be printed.

It wasn't exactly his field, but this much he understood: if the machine truly functioned, it promised to be a goldmine.

Whenever Orlov thought of Tasstain, he felt a twinge of uneasiness. With regard to the German company, he had no scruples, but it somehow bothered him to betray Tasstain and steal his invention. Because of his position he was unable to change anything. He had to make use of the documents. So many people already knew about them that there could be no turning back. The factory would be copied, as well as the production units, and the machine would be developed. No one would worry a bit about rights or obligations. After all, were these not the methods of capitalist enterprises?

Orlov arranged all the papers into an orderly package, stuffed it into his briefcase, and left his office. In ten minutes the final talks with Bugitchkov were due to take place. Agent No 14, responsible for the procurement of all the information, was also to attend the meeting.

☆   ☆   ☆

Dora Tasstain prayed for the first time in her life. Kovlenko had been the one to instruct her when she asked about how to pray. Man can speak with God, he said, because God knows all about our lives. He doesn't merely influence our doings but is the One who plans them. Whatever we may encounter in life comes from him if we allow him to be our authority.

That day Marc had told her of his plans to fly to Russia, and she was terribly worried about him. What would happen if the undertaking should fail? He might never come back. But in spite of the danger she did not oppose him, choosing rather, as Kovlenko had suggested, to discuss her worries with God. Maybe, if the necessity arose, he would work a miracle. For her husband a great deal was at stake. His job and his invention were his whole life, and she understood that he would not allow himself to be betrayed.

Within the company itself there was a certain undertone of alarm because of the involvement with Russia. No one was quite sure how to behave. Marc's first step was to cease all operations and ask his fellow directors to postpone decisions until they had discovered how the Russians would react. Once the documents were back in their own hands, they might be able to take other measures. The Russians would not dare to make trouble if they knew their secret schemes had been revealed. Perhaps in the end they could come to an agreement acceptable to both sides.

Since Silvia's departure for Moscow Dr Ott, Tasstain and Range had been spending time together planning 'Operation Border Flight'. They were waiting for Silvia's first call, which would be the signal for Tasstain to leave with Range for Finland near the Russian border, where they were to remain until her second call indicating she had the papers. Her responsibility would end once she had turned them over to Sorvas or Mike Tasstain and made arrangements for their delivery. She had taken with her three of Marc's suggestions for landing strips, which he had worked out with the aid of large scale maps of the area.

Afterwards, Silvia was to fly back to Germany, leaving the transport of the papers up to Mike and Sorvas. Throughout the entire operation Dr Ott was to act as intermediary at home.

☆   ☆   ☆

When Silvia left the meeting with Bugitchkov and Orlov, she was carrying the files in her bag. Orlov had given them to her so that she could add the last bits of information that she said she had brought with her. She had twenty-four hours before she was due to return the completed files to Orlov.

First, she made contact with Sorvas and asked him to arrange a meeting as quickly as possible with the 'Stranger' Mike Tasstain. It was not easy to convince Mike. He had been in the secret service far too long to trust her lightly. She could just as easily be working for both sides in order to uncover his or Sorvas's work with the Christians. For this reason he had her describe the entire plan down to every last detail and asked her precise questions, in order to discover as much as possible.

Mike Tasstain held a position high up in the KGB administration. He had given up his own name after the plane crash years before, when he was thought to have been killed. After changing his identity, he made no effort to contact his friends and family in Germany, with the exception of his wife. But even she did not know he was a go-between for the CIA.

Mike Tasstain, alias Major Tukov, owed his position and rank, and his ability to survive, to his icy nerves and keen intuition. His one weakness was his sympathy for the German minorities, who were constantly oppressed because of their Christian beliefs. Here he was not able to suppress his heritage, and his wife, who belonged to the Christian underground movement, was able to influence him to help these brave soldiers of the cross whenever their distress was too great.

Of course, his obligations to the CIA conflicted with his duties in the upper echelons of the KGB. For a long time he had been a thorn in the flesh of his official colleagues, but his position had remained unaffected. With nerves as cold as a Siberian winter and a steely self-control, he was driven by a silent contempt for the Soviet terrorist regime. He constantly found occasion to dispose of his rivals and for this became the most feared man in the KGB.

But the constant tension under which he was forced to live was taking its toll. In spite of his icy exterior, his nerves were wearing thin, and he sensed that the day would come when he would have to relinquish his role if he were to survive. Many times he had toyed with the idea of leaving the Soviet Union, but since it would be impossible to take his wife with him, he never pursued the matter.

Now, with the discovery of his brother's plan, he was struck with the idea that this might be a good opportunity to leave the country secretly. Up to the moment that he delivered the papers there would be no problem for him. With his official car he would be able to pass all control points. It would be necessary, however, to get rid of the tail which even he had to put up with.

That evening, Silvia phoned Dr Ott: 'The flowers have been picked up and will be sent on their way. Tomorrow we'll meet in the garden.'

Early the next morning the Cessna set off from Germany in the direction of Helsinki, where it landed five hours later at the international airport, just in time for Marc to welcome the scheduled flight from Moscow with Silvia Schmitz on board. To avoid the risks of carrying any incriminating documents, she had memorised all the necessary information and was able to travel with only her handbag.

As soon as she and Tasstain were able to find a secluded spot, she gave him all the details he needed: the landing site, its distance from the military airport, the direction from which Sorvas and his brother would come. In addition, she gave him further information on air traffic between Finland and the Soviet Union and on patrol flights of the Russian air force in this area.

Marc calculated that as long as they stayed under the radar belt nothing could happen to them, in theory at least. The meeting point lay 150 miles from the border. To get there he would need twenty-five to thirty minutes. He allowed another thirty minutes for landing, delivery, and take-off, and then thirty minutes for the return flight. Not wanting to fly over the border at the same spot, he planned to chart a more northerly course and land in Turku, as if he had just come from Helsinki. From there he would head home to Germany.

Altogether the prospects looked fairly good. He knew he would be entering the lion's den and it would be up to him to get out again. He convinced himself that nothing untoward would take place. In any case, in thirty-six hours he would know. By then the mission would be over – one way or the other.

☆   ☆   ☆

Major Tukov's dark limousine approached the first control point on the arterial road between Leningrad and Moscow. Sorvas sat behind the wheel in the

111

leather-coat dress of a KGB man, with the obligatory hat. In the back sat Major Tukov and his wife. She was in army uniform, which did not fit her quietly modest person, but such formalities made it look official. The major too was dressed as a KGB official.

He coldly eyed the soldier controlling their papers, then handed him his identification: 'On a special mission to Leningrad.'

'Good. You may pass!' The soldier handed back his papers and saluted respectfully, nodded briefly to the major's wife, then signalled for the bar to be lifted.

As the official car continued on its course, Tukov made his report back to KGB headquarters: '1520 hours. Major Tukov with assistant on the way to Leningrad, control point 17.' Twenty minutes later this report lay on Bugitchkov's desk. He was in charge of keeping track of all KGB traffic. What made him wonder was Tukov's assistant.

Always looking for any opportunity to trip up the major, Bugitchkov maintained a special interest in all his activities. Even a disciplined agent like Tukov could slip once.

He picked up the phone and called the next control point Tukov would have to pass on his way to Leningrad.

'I need a personal description of the individual accompanying Tukov – of course, without causing any upset.'

Mike Tasstain, alias Major Tukov, had by now turned off the route to Leningrad, which had been given as a diversion. Sorvas, who knew most of the uncontrolled roads and streets, drove northwest, always using detours to get to their true destination.

When Tukov failed to show up at the next control point, Bugitchkov's suspicions were confirmed, and he concluded that something unscheduled was taking place. Immediately he ordered all street controls to report the passing of the official car bearing Tukov and his companion. Aware that he could face discipline if the major learned of his actions, he was nevertheless goaded by such hatred of his arch-rival that he threw caution to the winds and dared to hope that his distrust would pay off.

After waiting for two hours with nervous anticipation, he received information that led him to believe Tukov was heading for the Finnish border. According to the description, the woman must be his wife. The driver could not be identified. There were no black-bearded men among the KGB chauffeurs.

Bugitchkov sensed his big chance. He got in touch with his agent on the border and ordered all street control points there to position a plain-clothes KGB guard, who was to keep his eyes open and report any incidents to headquarters. Then he warned all border airports to be on the alert and demanded regular reports on movements in the border area. It would not be the first time a top KGB officer tried to take off for the West via Finland.

The telephone rang. 'Bugitchkov, is that you? This is Orlov speaking! Do you have any idea where agent 14 is? She was supposed to come around this morning with the documents on the German factory, but she's disappeared. Her superior officer said she had ordered a flight to Helsinki.'

'To Helsinki, you said? And she didn't report to anyone before leaving? I don't like this at all. I'll check around and find out if anyone has seen her. If so, I'll notify you.'

Soon he had a description of all the passengers on the scheduled flight out of Moscow. Silvia had been among them, but she had no baggage with her, which certainly looked very suspicious. Bugitchkov immediately dialled Orlov's number.

'No 14 is in Helsinki. If I'm not wrong, there's something funny going on. I'll have her office and apartment searched directly.'

Unable to fit all the pieces together as yet, Bugitchkov smelled the threatening scandal. He ordered his people in Helsinki to find Silvia. If necessary he would bring her back by force. Then he set off for her apartment. He wanted to be there himself when the search was conducted.

☆ ☆ ☆

As Marc hurried around his plane making the final visual checks, he congratulated himself for having picked that olive-green colour. In his low flight over the border, it might well serve as camouflage. As always before a long flight, he had a hollow feeling in the pit of his stomach, an anxiety of which others were unaware except when he pressed his eyes closed. But usually it disappeared as soon as he had settled down behind the controls of his plane and reported to the tower that he was ready to go.

Today he had run through everything twice, meticulously checking off every item on his list. If anything was to go wrong on this mission, he wanted to assure himself it would not be due to mechanical defects or technical errors.

To calm his fears, he told himself this was just another ordinary flight and forced himself to compare it to his first low flights over his home airport. He remembered flying close to the ground in figure-eights, using trees as markers. He recalled skimming over fields in simulated forced landings. Today, like any professional pilot, he would have preferred to fly higher, but he was glad of his early experiences, which might just come in handy.

Tasstain felt around in his travel bag for the leather-covered flask and took a swallow of brandy. Then he prepared himself for flight, started up the engine, and switched on his controls, taking the microphone in his hands.

'Helsinki ground control, this is DENMI. Request runway clearance for visual flight to Turku.'

As he throttled forward, the flight chart lay across his knees, folded so that he could readily make out Helsinki and his course over the border and back again. He had divided the flight into one-minute intervals, marking significant points and any alternative turn-offs he might be forced to use.

As he cleared the runway and the airport dropped off behind him, his fears likewise fell away, and he felt exhilarated. Unconsciously gritting his teeth, he set the plane on course, glancing briefly at the chart to double-check his route. Now the important task was to follow the planned route. As in the war, the clock was ticking, and whoever went by it and was lucky came back.

Lucky? Was that the right word for him? Did he still count on luck and coincidence? A faint smile crossed his lips. No, no longer did luck and coincidence play a role in his life. Now he depended on God, and those whom God directed.

Since his trip to Moscow and his participation in the services of the underground congregation, and particularly after his traumatic experience in prison, he had come to a personal relationship with God. He had been worried and shaken till suddenly he had realised that there was not simply a God but *his* God. Kovlenko and Range had been able to help him strengthen his belief, and now he knew that that had been the turning point in his life.

Marc left his altitude and descended to 500 feet. It was six in the evening and another thirty miles to the Russian border. He flew even lower until he was virtually hugging the forest. At first it was difficult to stay low and follow the contours of the hills and obstacles in his path. But gradually, with each new ridge and valley it became easier. Out of radio range at that elevation, he had to rely strictly on his compass and time calculations. The clock ticked off the time: only five more minutes to the Russian border.

He trimmed the engine as precisely as possible, to achieve maximum efficiency. At his altitude it was very important. As he twisted around this crest and down that dale, he imagined that the craft was magnetically guided by the contours of the earth's surface. The thought passed quickly as he guided the plane over the next ridge. All his concentration was needed to chart a course between the invisible radar net above him and the uneven but all too solid earth below. His charts were helpful, but visual alertness was indispensable.

He had charted a route over unoccupied territory, especially beyond the border. But what was marked as uninhabited on a map was not necessarily so in reality. There were probably a few observation points hidden within the border area for which Marc had to keep a lookout.

According to his watch, he would be crossing the border at any moment. He was able to make out the shaven stretch of land and the fence delineating the border, then a heavily forested area. Suddenly a barely visible road appeared beneath him. Making a sharp sweeping turn to the left, he was able to follow its path with his eye for a brief second, just long enough to notice a cloud of dust in the distance – most likely a car. Though at that low altitude he could not be detected on the radar screen, a ground patrol would have no trouble spotting him.

There was no time to think of consequences while occupied with watching the terrain, flying the craft, and maintaining the course plotted on the chart.

He counted each passing minute while keeping his eye fixed on the area below: forest...clearing ...forest...hills...road...forest. Subconsciously he registered the wisps of cloud above and the fact that neither rain nor fog was in sight. Passing the seventeenth minute, he came to a long lake. He pressed the nose even lower and imagined he could feel the dampness of the water on his belly. A boat appeared out of nowhere, and he could make out two people staring up at him. Then the shore was under his wings. He pulled up over the trees and climbed over the next hill.

The twenty-third minute. Daylight was dimming. The sky was getting cloudy. As he skimmed another hill, he let up on the fuel a bit. This must be the last valley before the landing point that lay ahead of him. Still more woods, then a river.

The twenty-eighth minute. He turned in the direction of the charted landing strip, that was described as a long straight path in a field. It had to lie beyond the next cluster of trees. Just as his eyes cleared the trees and spotted the path, he caught sight of the helicopter. It was flying in the same direction, only higher.

☆   ☆   ☆

Sorvas, too, saw the helicopter and without a moment's hesitation veered off the road into the woods. With not a second to spare, he was just able to escape being noticed by the flying patrol. The car crackled in the underbrush, then sank into the muddy ground beneath, hopelessly stuck.

'If we run through the field and the next patch of woods, we should come out at the right spot,' Sorvas urged.

'Do you think we'll make it on time?'

'He agreed to wait there half an hour.'

With no time to think it over, Mike Tasstain seized

his bag out of the car. 'Good, let's go! There's no turning back now.' He grabbed his wife by the arm and led her behind him into the clearing.

Sorvas heaved the suitcase on to his shoulder and hurried after them. It was a long field they had to cross over. If the helicopter appeared before they were able to reach the protection of the woods ahead, they would be lost. For Mike and his wife there really was no turning back. Sorvas would have no problem getting away. Besides, he had friends who would let him lie low for a while until everything had blown over. But for the other two, everything was at stake.

At the last control point they had noticed that someone suspected something. Why else the plain-clothes officers? They had been detained for quite some time and were required to show all their papers. How fortunate that Mike had had the papers issued so meticulously and was able to give precise answers to all their questions. Control was obliged to let them pass, if only for the reason that Major Tukov was a feared name. But something was going on, that they knew. The helicopter was proof enough.

In the middle of the field the three heard the sound of an engine coming toward them through the air.

'Is that the helicopter returning?' Sorvas gasped.

'Get down!' Mike shouted.

☆   ☆   ☆

When he spotted the helicopter Marc had no choice: he had to land immediately. With his air speed he could be easily overtaken. Turning back was out of the question. In any case, the rendezvous point was close by. The worst that could happen was that he would have to go by foot through the woods to the designated spot. The only important thing at the moment was to get out of sight of the flight patrol.

Below him he spied a long field. That was where he would have to land. Fuel off, prop in, flaps out, landing gear down. In a sharp sweep he pulled the craft over the edge of the wood and glided on to the field, observing as he levelled off that it had not been ploughed. Suddenly he sighted the three cowering on the ground ahead of him, directly in his landing path.

'Get up! Get out of the way – just a couple of yards!' he heard himself hiss over the sound of the propeller.

Sorvas was the first to recognise the plane. 'It's him!' he shouted. 'Move!' He pushed the other two. 'Get over to the woods, quick!'

Marc set down, bounced once, then dug two deep tracks with his wheels, coming to a halt at the edge of the woods. His brother was the first to accost him.

'They're patrolling the area with a helicopter. Did they see you?' he gasped.

'I'm not sure – but I spotted the helicopter. That's why I was forced to land here – and what a stroke of luck!'

Sorvas came up panting, with the heavy suitcase in tow. 'You'll have to leave immediately. They can return any minute and will know everything.'

There was no time for conversation. Marc ripped open the baggage compartment and threw the bag and suitcase inside.

'Do you have the documents?'

'They're in the bag.'

Marc turned to the woman in uniform, but before he could ask any questions, Mike said quietly, 'We're coming along too. This is my wife.'

With a quick handshake Marc urged her into the back seat of the plane, with Mike behind. 'Buckle up!' he commanded, then turned to Sorvas.

'I'll be staying here. God be with you!'

Marc was already at the controls. With an understanding nod, he edged the throttle forward. The plane moved slowly on to the open field. Since the ground was obviously soft, he would require double the distance to gather speed for take-off. For the first time he regretted not having better wheels, since his seemed to dredge their way over the damp earth. With two extra passengers aboard, the plane was agonisingly slow in picking up speed. Ever so slightly, Marc leaned forward, as one might on horseback. The woods ahead crowded the distance. He tugged on the elevator control. The plane was not yet ready for lift-off, but at least the nose responded to the signal.

The craft continued to gather speed. Then, with a practised eye, Marc knew that if he were to make it over the trees it had to be *now*. Pulling back on the wheel, he felt the sweet conquest of winged machine as, released from the tug of earth and grass, it lurched forward into air. Behind rose a huge cloud of surface dust. For mere seconds he kept the nose down to pick up speed, then pulled up and away, just clearing the pines that threatened to snare the fragile craft.

Again he sighted the helicopter, this time coming directly at him. There was only one way to go – up, up into the massing clouds, his only means of escape. Soon, he knew, there would be a whole swarm on his tail. The cloud bank hung at 3,000 feet. He checked his altitude at 1,000 feet, but his speed was good. Before his adversary could tell which direction he was taking, he swept past, shooting an upward curve in the direction of the clouds.

The helicopter immediately altered course and followed in full pursuit. The gap between them narrowed. Low cloud had never looked so welcome....

A sudden burst of machine-gun fire sent a searing message to the three hapless civilians. Marc felt the shot sink in as the plane shuddered. The clouds were getting closer. He was still flying, the engine continued its steady climb, he himself was unhurt.

Looking back over his shoulder, he saw his brother slumped over the lap of his wife. A red blotch was spreading over her skirt. She looked up with frightened eyes, just as they went into the cloudbank.

Marc had no time to take care of his passengers. His first priority was to fly the plane to safety, relying on instrument navigation. As long as they were obscured by clouds they were relatively safe, and he figured that the border must be fairly close by now. His watch told him they had been flying towards the west for fifteen minutes.

As if in a trance, Natasha had removed her jacket and placed it over Mike, who by now had lost consciousness. Unable to do any more for him, she leaned forward.

'How much longer will it take?'

Marc had already picked up radio Turku. 'We ought to make it in twenty minutes.'

☆   ☆   ☆

As Silvia entered the train for Turku, she knew with the sensitivity of a secret agent that she was being tailed. Though not personally acquainted with her KGB colleagues stationed in Finland, she concluded that someone from their ranks was keeping an eye on her. She had already assumed that after her sudden disappearance from Moscow, along with the papers, her superiors would suspect foul play. No doubt they were at this very moment busily engaged in trying to find out what was going on.

She took a seat in a fairly full compartment and hid behind a paper. Her mind raced on. What if

121

something had happened to Sorvas or the Tasstain brothers? The authorities would then be on to something big. This much she knew: Bugitchkov would certainly put two and two together. He was no fool. In that case, she would have to assume that they would try to get rid of her. For the moment, at least, her safety lay in not being alone.

Caught in a scheme of international proportions, she had to be on her toes. Her trip to Turku was for the purpose of preventing any KGB plots on the arrival of the plane. Stepping off the train, she mingled with the crowd and at the last minute hopped on a bus to the airport.

A number of faces could have belonged to her pursuers, but she was unable to pinpoint any for sure. She tried to memorise as many as possible, for future reference. One never knew. Arranging to be the last off, she didn't head for the arrival gates but entered a side door, which she hoped would lead to the control tower. She wanted to find out if Tasstain was on his way to Turku, and the air traffic controllers would be the first to know.

She ran down a long hall, past doors labelled Flight Security, Weather Information, Airport Control. Slipping through the door to the tower, she glanced back just in time to see a big blond man in uniform enter the door at the far end of the hall. In her urgency she took the stairs two at a time. From above she heard typewriters clicking, and radio transmissions crackling with flight data.

Gasping for breath as she burst into the skylit sanctuary, she made a quick apology, adding, 'I'm expecting someone arriving in a private plane. Could you tell me if one is en route from Helsinki?'

The official sized her up critically. 'We've just received a message from a German plane asking to land in ten minutes. The pilot ordered an ambulance

122

and a doctor. He said they had a fatally wounded person on board. Look, there's the ambulance in front of the hall.'

Outside it had already grown dark. The circling searchlight was all she could see. Pulling herself together, she asked calmy, 'How can I get there?'

'Down the stairs and follow the signs marked 'Personnel Only,' he said – sympathetically, she felt.

Behind her the blond-haired uniformed man came through the door. Silvia turned on her heels, raced past him, and ran downstairs.

'What did the pretty young lady want?' he asked casually. The official, noting the captain's stripes, explained to him what Silvia had asked.

Before Tasstain landed, Silvia wanted to make a quick phone call to Dr Ott. He would want to know that Marc was safely across the border. She hastily dialled the number and was connected immediately.

'They're on their way but Mike Tasstain seems to be injured. They'll be landing shortly. I want to be there. I thought you should be the first to know. That's why I called!'

'Praise God, my dear. Come home quickly!' There was a click and then the dialling tone ended the brief conversation.

'Come home soon,' he had said. How good that sounded! Caught in a moment of pleasure, she remained standing next to the phone. All of a sudden she experienced a pang of conscience. Wasn't it her fault that Marc had set off on such a perilous journey? Why hadn't she given up her job a long time ago? She might have been able to prevent not only this but many other acts of injustice on the part of the Soviets. If only she could make up for what she had so ruthlessly done to make others unhappy.

Outside she saw that the ambulance was parked next to a Cessna. Two men were carrying the stretcher around to the plane. A woman was also there. Then she noticed the blond officer heading in their direction. It struck her that he had not wanted her, but Major Tukov. In a flash she realised the danger and ran towards the plane.

'Watch out!' she cried to Marc. 'The captain!'

They would stop at nothing to get Tukov, she knew that. In the dark she stumbled over a cable but recovered quickly and continued running. The blond captain increased his speed. He too had grasped what was going on.

Marc, hearing Silvia's cry, ran to block the captain's path. Two ambulance men had the unconscious body of Mike on the stretcher and were moving to the rear of the ambulance. The captain shoved Marc to one side and reached inside his jacket pocket. As he aimed at the stretcher, Silvia jumped in front of him. The gun went off. Marc threw himself upon the assassin, and the airfield came alive.

The men in the tower viewing the drama sprang into action. Spotlights came on, lighting up the airfield, and the plane and ambulance were quickly surrounded. The captain, whom Marc had momentarily knocked out, was arrested.

Only then did Marc notice Silvia lying on the ground. Natasha knelt down next to her and for the second time that day cushioned a head in her lap.

'The blond man,' Silvia whispered, 'he's from the KGB. Watch out for them. They'll leave no stone unturned. Stay with your husband at all times in the hospital.' Exhausted, she laid her head back, breathing heavily. Then her words came out unevenly as she mustered her last ounce of strength. 'Tell Dr Ott his love helped to turn me from my wrong path. He can remember me that way. Do you think I could have made up for all I've done?'

124

'Oh, yes,' Natasha said. 'You've done much the same as Christ did. He sacrificed himself not for one man only but for the whole human race and made up for their sins. Have faith in him and you won't have to worry about your past or future any more.'

Silvia closed her eyes. Yes, now she was able to accept it all. It was so easy. She saw her misspent life behind her and the Man on the cross before her and knew that she was in good, caring hands.

As the attendants lifted her on to the second stretcher and placed her in the ambulance, her face wore a serene smile.

☆   ☆   ☆

Agent 14 died on the way to the hospital. Mike Tasstain, following emergency surgery, made a good recovery. As soon as he was out of danger, he and his wife were taken back to Germany by helicopter, under police protection.

Marc Tasstain had to submit to prolonged questioning. Although he had the sympathy of his interrogators, he was forced to pay bail before being allowed to return to Germany. The Finnish authorities were obviously expecting a complaint from the Soviets about Tasstain's violation of border regulations. The complaint never came. Apparently the incident was too embarrassing to risk official notice. The Russians acted as if nothing had happened.

Nor did the construction of the printing factory take place. There were talks between the Ministry of Economy in Moscow and the Foreign Trade Bureau in Germany, ending in cancellation of the contract because of technical difficulties.

In Moscow, the incident and above all the disappearance of Tukov resulted in a wave of official purges, to which Orlov and Bugitchkov were to fall victim; both disappeared into the Siberian Gulag. The KGB apparently failed to uncover the connection between Tasstain and the underground church movement.

☆　☆　☆

A few weeks after the fateful flight, Mike Tasstain's happy return was being celebrated in his brother's home. Everyone had gathered together – even Dr Ott, who had retreated into seclusion after Silvia's tragic death. After the meal, they all sat around the fireplace waiting for Kovlenko to read from the Bible.

'I've just received a letter from Sorvas, which I'd like to read to all of you,' the old man announced cheerfully. 'You'll probably understand it, although he had to write it partly in code.' Opening it up, he began reading:

> Dear friends in Germany! As I discovered, there still seem to be angels who make sure that in God's heaven, borders may be passed through and flown over. They are the same angels who, on my dangerous journey home, did not disappoint me either. I was sick for a long while and had to stay with friends, who, after my recovery, brought me back safe and sound to Moscow. We notice that K. is with you. Since he has been reporting on our situation to the West, we feel that things are improving. Many have been released from detention, and our congregations are growing. Also, we must not forget to mention how helpful your packages have been. Every time you pass on our message, those concerned breathe a bit easier. It is

truly a blessing how the authorities are reacting to the spread of news in the West. You cannot imagine how much it helps when you in the West dedicate yourselves to our cause of resistance against ideological repression. We believe in the God who himself died for us and not in 'gods' who allow others to die.

Best wishes, Sorvas and the underground church.'

Kovlenko set the letter down gently, picked up his Bible, and started reading a passage he particularly wanted to share on this night. 'Where can I go from your spirit? Where can I flee from your presence? If I go up to the heavens, you are there; if I make my bed in the depths, you are there. If I rise on the wings of the dawn, if I settle on the far side of the sea, even there your hand will guide me, your right hand will hold me fast' (Psalm 139:7-10).

For more information about the needs and ministry of Christian Missions to the Communist World and for additional copies of this book, please write:

In USA:
C.M.C.W.
P.O. Box 443
Bartlesville, OK 74005
USA

In Australia:
Rev. Merv Knight
C.M.C.W., P.O. Box 598
Penrith NSW
2750 Australia

In Canada:
Klaas Brobbel
J.T.T.C.W.
P.O. Box 117 Port Credit
Mississauga, Ontario
Canada L5G 4L5

In England:
Christian Missions
P.O. Box 19
Bromley Kent, BR1 1DJ
England

In New Zealand:
J.T.T.C.W.
P.O. Box 69-158
Glendene, Auckland 8
New Zealand